TX 2-444-112

THE SPY WHO FELL OFF
THE BACK OF A BUS

THE SPY WHO FELL OFF THE BACK OF A BUS

MARC LOVELL

A Crime Club Book
Doubleday
NEW YORK   LONDON   TORONTO   SYDNEY   AUCKLAND

A Crime Club Book
Published by Doubleday, a division of
Bantam Doubleday Dell Publishing Group, Inc.
666 Fifth Avenue, New York, New York 10103

Doubleday, Crime Club, and the portrayal of a man
with a gun are trademarks of Doubleday,
a division of Bantam Doubleday Dell Publishing
Group, Inc.

Library of Congress Cataloging-in-Publication Data
Lovell, Marc.
The spy who fell off the back of a bus / Marc Lovell. — 1st ed.
p. cm.
"A Crime Club novel."
I. Title.
PR6062.O853S6975   1988   88-11892
823′ .914—dc19   CIP
ISBN 0-385-24608-0
Copyright © 1988 by Marc Lovell
All Rights Reserved
Printed in the United States of America
October 1988
First Edition
OG

THE SPY WHO FELL OFF
THE BACK OF A BUS

ONE

Harlequin Mansions, Bloomsbury, was a haughty-faced building of Edwardian birth. In one of its apartments Virginia Woolf was reputed to have spent the afternoon asleep on a couch, a story every tenant had scoffed at until informed in confidence by the landlord, when he came to raise the rent, that not only was it true, but the newly evaluated flat was the very one in which it had happened.

Apple, kind, kept his smile on the inside of his mouth if fellow tenants dropped the Woolf name in proprietory fashion, as though it were something they had on the mantelpiece. His own apartment was the one in question, he knew. He got told so under profane oath every time he raised the rent of his own accord. This happened whenever he felt that his enjoyment of his guilt at the rising cost of living was reaching morbid proportions.

However, the prompter to action wasn't guilt, Apple preferred to believe, but rather the need to be assured about the Woolf connexion. And true it was that, proud of his reticence, he relished never mentioning to anyone his flat's celebrity. When, in that murmurous voice used by name-droppers and invalids, people told of owning, say, a chair which had once been sat in by Stephane Grappelli, Apple merely said, "How interesting." He said it with a downswoop of his upper body—

to show he wasn't just saying that, he assumed, in reality it was to hide his face in case it should be displaying sympathy.

Appleton Porter had a pale, freckled, bland-featured face. What it lacked in character it made up for in sensitivity, no stranger to the wince, the blanch, the quiver and, in sad particular, the blush.

Help in the form of distraction came from neither his gingery hair nor sober clothing, both neat to a tedious degree, which state Apple would have changed like a shot if only he had owned the courage. He told himself this often, even while being convinced of his bravery and knowing that respectable philologists weren't supposed to look like actors or bookies.

Fortunately, Apple's face had the double aspect that we realise our friends have always had when they let us down. It was loyal as well as treacherous. Positive emotions it showed off like clean and clever children, giving a garnish to the smile, striking sparks in the green eyes, eliminating the blandness. When pleased, Appleton Porter was attractive.

He became so now, suddenly, as in approaching Harlequin Mansions at a stride he lowered his gaze from the upper windows. He felt a lurch in his stomach, a smile cut gladly into freckles, he tightened all over with excitement and Ginny went out of his mind.

Causation was a small, scruffy older man with uncouth features. Standing on the front steps, he wore a blue boiler suit and ex-white trainers. He could have passed for a janitor who wonders anxiously which way to go for the jog he's convinced isn't going to do him any good.

Apple slowed. From obliquely across the street, grey with an English summer evening's damp chill, he looked at Albert and fought against letting his excitement get out of rein. After all, he cautioned, there could be many reasons for fetid Albert's appearance here.

That Apple couldn't think of one single reason, bar the hysterical, served reversely to bring a measure of calm: he needed to be cool, sharp, the calculating pro, if this is what it seemed.

Jaw severe, Apple picked up speed. He crossed the road and came to an efficient halt in front of where the small man stood in an insolent slouch. They were eye-to-eye. Albert was on the top step, but Appleton Porter was six feet seven inches tall.

In a cockney accent you could have cut with aitches and still not understood, were you not from the region or a linguist, Albert said, "You're late, mate, case you're interested."

"Somehow," Apple said primly, "I was not aware of having an engagement."

"What I meant, see, clever bollocks, was it's supposed to take you eleven minutes to drive here from that there place in Kensington."

That there place was the United Kingdom Philological Institute, where Apple served as a senior official. "You're a bit out-of-date," he said. "Nowadays, with advances in traffic planning, it takes sixteen minutes."

"I'm not a bit out of nothink, me. I only know what I'm told."

"And no doubt if I stand here long enough I, too, will be told something."

Albert straightened from the gangster slouch. His expression changing from average unpleasant to veiled menace, he said, "Careful, lanky shanks. Get shirty with me and I might just forget why I'm here." He knew his power.

Remembering that he was brave, Apple tried a bluff: "I expect Mr. Watkin won't mind the delay or an assumed noncontact."

Albert looked along the street and began to hum. Apple, taking the steps in one long stride, went to the entrance, where he paused. Albert continued humming.

It was more to end his mental hum-along with the tune than to give in, he told himself, that Apple turned and asked, humbly, "Do you have a message for me?"

When after another chorus Albert broke off the hum, it was to say, "No."

"Oh."

"What I got for you, mate, is a order."

"Thank you," Apple said. "What is it?"

"You're to come with me at once."

"Ready when you are."

Albert went down the steps on, "Follow me, and let's hope nobody gets the idea we're together." He chuckled.

As Apple began to follow, he tried to think of a witty, biting, devastating retort. Nothing came, though he knew by drab experience that he would land a beauty when he was getting ready for bed.

In compensation as he continued tailing along the street, Apple smiled whimsically at the shimmying of the boiler suit. He might have trodden on Albert's heels if it weren't for accepting how cheap and easy that one was, as well as the fact of the older man's genius at unarmed combat.

Albert stopped. He was beside a man whose ordinariness was matched by the car he had just stopped leaning on. Sheepishly the stranger said, "We're out of luck."

Albert: "What you mean?"

"Battery's gone flat. She won't start."

Whereas at any other time this would have caused Apple discomfort, as did all occurrences that punctured the romantic view he held of his secret trade, now he grinned as searingly as a cat at a lame dog.

With a lazy about-face he drawled, "I have wheels nearby. Come along, Albert."

The older man said a feeble, "Well . . ."

Walking, Apple added, If you can keep up, with those little leggies of yours. The addition, however, was silent, made in that political compartment of the mind where, in order for points to be scored, truth and matters of consequence are treated like failed cavaliers. Elsewhere Apple would no more have thought than said what would not only have been to the recipient a brutal insult, the kind he had lifelong had to suffer, but also a mocking jibe at his own desires. No lover of his stature, Apple wouldn't at all have minded owning little leggies himself.

The gloom's robust melodrama appealed to Apple as he led Albert across the underground parking garage. It went with his simmer of excitement, his anticipation of adventures to come. Had he been alone, he might have whistled something baleful in a low key, to josh it all. He contented himself with sending ahead to Ethel an elaborate wink.

Ethel, in her slot by the back wall, looked middle-aged instead of old because of her outrageous flashy paint-job, fine on a buggy but odd on a traditional London taxi. For Apple, who saw her as beautiful, Ethel may well have been his sole act of defiance against the stultifying correctness of his everyday world.

Once in the driver's seat, Apple tensed, as you would in semi-expectation of a slap. He felt sure that Albert, getting in the back, would close the door with a slam.

All Apple heard, however, was a gentle click. Relaxing, he realised he ought to have known that even cretinesque Albert would show respect for a veteran colleague.

Ethel had been an undercover vehicle all her life, until forced into retirement, too old-fashioned to pass any longer as a working taxi, at which juncture Apple had become her owner. Starting with the regular police, she had loaned style to several law agencies before gracing for twenty years a department of British Intelligence referred to as Upstairs.

Apple had worked for the same department for half that time, since leaving university. Yet during his service he had been sent out into the field as an agent only on rare occasions, a tourist in spyland. His main contribution to the cloak-and-dagger trade was through his skill at languages. He spoke so many that when asked the number, he usually gave it as seven or eight so people wouldn't think him a liar or a braggart.

For Upstairs and on loan to other departments, Apple did translations, wrote letters and checked decoded messages for nuance, he acted as interpreter at interrogations, at debriefings and at gatherings of Western secret service people when they were pretending not to distrust one another.

The work was sometimes interesting, mostly a bore. It was not why Apple had allowed himself to be recruited. What he had expected, and hoped for still, was action: the gasp and gallop of adventure, the mystery and intrigue of foreign parts, the temptation and danger of sultry women. These he had found in abundance, but inside the covers of his favourite reading, espionage fiction. In real life he seemed to be forever waiting for the call.

Apple numbered among the Upstairs people known as the faceless ones, a peculiar breed with often peculiar abilities. If Angus Watkin wanted a man who could throw up at will or a girl with a moustache, a person of awesome girth or a woman who knew how to knit with her feet, Angus Watkin had one on call. The faceless specialists were not exactly overworked.

Apple knew why, in his own case, he wasn't used more often in the field, even though speak-freaks were frequently needed. Partly it was on account of some of the marks he had scored during training at Damian House:

Languages 10, Security Clearance 10, Unarmed Combat 6, Acting Ability 6, Lying Ability 6, Resistance to Physical Pain 5, Resistance to Mental Stress 9, General Knowledge 9, Marksmanship 7, Tolerance for Alcohol 5.

Partly his lack of undercover work was because of his height. A man of six-seven, Apple was forced to agree, had little hope of success at the dimming of presence, the vital need to become one of the passing herd.

Partly nonemployment was due to past performance. He had not shone especially when Angus Watkin, his Control, had included him in a caper, although Apple had stated to his own satisfaction that colleagues were equally to blame. Said statement had been made at home in writing and the paper then eaten.

Partly his being ignored was because of three bad habits. The first was that of collecting useless information, which was thought to make for absent-mindedness; the second was that of feeling sympathetic toward others, who might happen to be on the opposite side; the third was that of blushing.

There was as much hope of his personality drawbacks lessening, never mind disappearing, Apple well knew, as there was of him losing a foot in height. He would always be a faceless one. Fat chance he had of actually going Upstairs, wherever it might be. He would continue as before, if lucky enough to be summoned, meeting his Control in odd corners in and around the city; corners which, as though in compensation, tended to be salubrious, inviting, even glamorous. Angus Watkin's malice was not one hundred percent pure, Apple sometimes allowed.

It was a junkshop. Albert pointed it out to Apple as they walked along the seedy commercial street from where Ethel had been parked. Their position side by side was due to Apple's guilt. He had been thinking, unavoidably, about the dead-battery agent.

It could have been the poor bastard's first piece of business for Upstairs, Apple saw. It could have been his comeback job after a lay-off for some blunder. It could have been a test to see how he would handle the minor emergency.

Apple pictured Dead-Battery waiting throughout the day for his bout of action, nervous, pacing, not being able to eat a bite, chain-smoking, telling himself what a great job he was going to make of this deal, smiling as he . . .

Albert, first cousin today to Dead-Battery's flop, had been allowed to catch up in order to keep Apple's simmer of excitement at a reasonable level, Apple believed.

"What?" he asked.

"That shop."

"The one with the old bathtubs outside?"

"Right," Albert said dejectedly. "In and through to the back." He stopped walking. "So long."

His desire to offer a consoling handshake countered by the reminder that pro agents didn't do that sort of thing, Apple strode on. He hoped Albert wouldn't waste too many future hours in thinking up vengeful, awful cracks to make when next they met. Not for the first time this week, Apple felt glad he was not neurotic.

He went in the shop. Its silent desertion being acceptable, he sought embellishment in wending a path through heaped flotsam by lowering his eyelids a ways. The plebian became mysterious, the pathetic sublime.

Presently, after rounding a stuffed lion that was giraffe from the shoulders up, Apple reached a junction, where stood a pillar of telephone directories. He had gone by when the pillar spoke. In a dull voice it said, "Porter."

Apple doubled back, eyes normal. The lioraffe, he saw, was a bent lamp-post standing in a hamper; the pile of directories was Angus Watkin.

"Good evening, sir," Apple said.

His Control asked, "Is this a new habit of yours, Porter, walking about with your eyes closed?"

"I was giving them a second's rest, actually."

"Do you know how many priceless objets d'art have been found in junkshops?"

"Thousands, I suppose, sir."

"So few," Angus Watkin said, "that they wouldn't take up the fingers of one hand."

Apple said, "Yes, sir."

His Control was one of those Neithers. They're known to all detectives, who in questioning witnesses about a suspect (tall or short, young or old, stout or slim) receive a repeat, "Neither." In the super category, bland on bland, Angus Watkin wore a raincoat that could be seen as soiled fawn or clean brown, had no expression on his forgettable face and would have fitted to perfection anywhere among Caucasians as your friendly neighborhood nonentity.

He said, "But to the nub, Porter. Which is that I am going to send you on a little errand."

That being spookspeak for an assignment of consequence, Apple was able to dismiss his anticipation as redundant, which let his excitement settle, abate in satisfaction. He said a quiet, "Well now."

"You do, I understand, possess two or three languages."

You know precisely how many I have to the last verb, Apple mused, just as you know almost everything there is about me that you might consider useable. He nodded.

Watkin asked, "But can you speak the French used in Quebec?"

"I can duplicate that patois perfectly, sir."

"And can you, Porter, speak English with the Canadian accent of that region?"

"Fairly well."

"You'll be given coaching."

With a reassuring clench of one cheek Apple said, "A week's all I'd need."

"You'll get two days."

"Sounds like an emergency, sir."

Watkin said, "Your possible use in this endeavour came up only within the hour."

Which ruled out Dead-Battery having spent the day painfully awaiting his flop, Apple thought in relief. He asked, "How many of us will there be in the team, sir?"

"No teams, Porter. You will be totally on your own. The mission is yours."

Lifting a hand to pat his face briefly, calmingly, Apple said in a pale voice, "I shall do my utmost to justify the confidence you are placing in me."

His Control stared at him for a moment before saying, "Yes."

"So I have a number-name," Apple stated.

"It, from this point on, is One."

"Thank you, sir."

"I'm not the one to thank, Porter. Your selection was made by computer. Its choice was based on height first, language second, ability third, experience fourth."

"Height, sir?"

"The man you will be impersonating is six feet five inches tall in his socks."

"My height exactly," Apple said.

Angus Watkin, ignoring him: "The fact of you being taller than that by two inches can be accommodated."

"Impersonation, did you say, sir?"

"I did."

"In Canada?"

"The where and why you will learn in due course," Angus Watkin said, showing disapproval the way flies make noisy landings. "For the time being please try to concentrate on absorbing for your role."

"Yes, sir," Apple said crisply. He began to follow as Angus Watkin moved slowly off along a path. They passed a pile of broken bird cages that made Apple sniff with victory and a mattress rolled in despair that made him give his attention back to Watkin. He looked away again demurely on noting that his chief was going thin at the crown.

"From here on," Watkin said, "your public name is Walter Brent. That nice straightforward name is the sanest thing about you."

"I'm crazy?"

"Eccentric. You frequently wear disguises. At the age of thirty-five you have been married four times. Every year you give a million dollars or so to charities which, to understate, are bizarre. You go to enormous lengths to avoid publicity, and of course you hate the press."

"I'm famous," Apple said cheerfully.

"No," his Control said. "Such as it is, your celebrity is limited to a particular strata of society. The man in the street has never heard of you. The popular press would be happy to splash you about, however, if there were ever a story to go with the wealth."

"If I can't be famous, I might as well be really loaded."

Over his shoulder Angus Watkin asked drably, "May I continue?"

"Sorry, sir."

"You, Walter Brent, are an expert on Enuit art, a connoisseur of fine cigars, a lover of antique tapestries. Also you collect old schooners, which you have airlifted to the private lake on your estate in northern Quebec province. You can't stand children or television, junk food or pop music. Obviously, you are not without intelligence and taste."

"Obviously," Apple said, following with a small laugh to cover his discomfort about children.

"Although your money, in the billions, was inherited,

you have handled it shrewdly and it continues to grow. Not uncommonly, your eccentricities stop at the bank door."

"I'm quite a character."

"You are," Angus Watkin said. He came to a slow halt, turned at the same speed. "I hope."

"Sir?"

"Can you, in fine, handle the role?"

"Absolutely, sir. Without a single doubt."

"Fortunately it's only for a few days. The real Walter Brent wouldn't be discovered to be elsewhere during that time."

Apple asked, "He doesn't know about this?"

"He does not," Watkin said. "So with the next forty-eight hours spent in preparation, you might be able to pull off this impersonation."

"Thank you, sir."

"If not the purpose of the mission."

"Which is what, sir? If I may ask."

"You may not," Angus Watkin said. "We must avoid overtaxing your mind at this point."

"Quite so," Apple said, as though he had been complimented.

"The purpose you will learn in due course, when you have learned to be Walter Brent."

"Agreed."

"To the best of your ability, at any rate."

"You won't be disappointed in me, sir."

Watkin's answer was to pronounce a name and a number. After his underling had repeated the address he said, "Go there now. Good-bye, One."

It was a quiet street in north-east London's vastness, where suburb after suburb compete in mediocrity and the police look disillusioned. The house, separated from its neighbours by at least one metre, had a new-painted neatness as well as a fetching garden.

Arrived by taxi from having taken Ethel home (here she would have stood out like a strawberry in fried onions), Apple had his knock answered by two groomed pretty women in their fifties. One addressed him in English with a Canadian accent, the other in Quebec French.

This system was to continue, with Apple responding to each in kind, as, starting in a comfortable living room, Agnes and Marie worked on building up for him a picture of Walter Brent.

The first photograph was a jolt. The eccentric billionaire bore no more resemblance to Appleton Porter than a cow does to a horse. But Apple didn't despond, knowing better than to think Angus Watkin could have made a mistake. A mathematician was more likely to get seven out of three plus three.

What Apple did do was decide that, as the women must surely knew the score, he would make a point of shrewdly worming out of them at least where the caper was set, if not its nature.

There were more photographs—man, home, estate, housekeeper and servants, surrounding landscape, nearest town. At the same time Agnes and Marie gave verbally a biographical outline and filled in on mannerisms of gesture, walk, speech. The women were gossipy rather than pedantic, casual instead of insistent. Apple absorbed.

Once he said, "Be nice to see Canada again."

Agnes said, "They have cheap package tours nowadays."

At times Apple was coached in passing. Put more slur

in it, he was told about his archaic French. For his English he heard, "More of a Scottish flavour on the '*ous*,' dear. It's 'oot' and 'aboot,' not 'out' and 'About.' "

After what Agnes called a slum banquet—sandwiches and shop cake—she took Apple off in a discreet car, still talking as she made a dubious job of driving. His body tense, Apple told himself not to knock it, this could be the caper's sole dose of danger.

In another lamplit suburb he enjoyed the alley they walked down, even though the door they entered led only to a shoe-repair workroom. The one person present in the aroma of leather strong enough to slip on and lace up, a middle-aged man in toeless slippers, took measurements: Apple's foot, including the distance between heel and ankle. He explained that he was making a pair of elastic-sided boots that would be imitation elevators.

Apple asked, "They'll look as if they've got heel-lifts inside but they won't have?"

Agnes reprimanded him for slipping out of accent; the man said, "Right, lad." Apple told one sorry, the other how nifty, himself that the lying boots would explain to observers why Walter Brent had become two inches taller—but what reason could be offered for Brent *wanting* to be, Apple didn't know. Such a desire was a stranger to his imagination.

As they drove toward the West End, Agnes told her gratifiedly nervous passenger about the financial pies in which the billionaire had fingers. Apple understood roughly a third of it.

He asked, "Is there anything you'd like me to send you from where I'm going?"

"No thank you, dear."

"Something peculiar to the region, perhaps?"

"There is nothing peculiar to the region," Agnes said. "Now let's find a place to park illegally. I love sending them tickets Upstairs."

Again they used a rear entrance. It was to a wigmaker's, which, Apple fancied, taking in the shelves of creations on wooden heads, looked like a courtroom with its public gallery filled with lawyers for a change, all rendered faceless by reason of having no parts to play.

The woman who sat Apple in a low, low chair was plain and brisk. His head she measured in every direction from the jaw up, making notes the while. Next she produced samples of hair, hanks of differing colour grades stuck on a rod.

Matching samples against Apple, the woman kept giving negative tuts. Whenever Agnes said, "That's perfect," she said, "Unfortunately," and Apple said, "I wouldn't dream of asking what's going on."

Relenting when she had found a suitable mismatch, the wigmaker told him, "We're creating for you a wig-and-beard ensemble. It's not supposed to look too real."

Apple nodded. He had the appearance part of it now. This was why facial resemblance was less important than stature. He would be hidden mostly behind hair, disguised as the eccentric Walter Brent in disguise.

From the wigmaker's they went to an East End warehouse. The man in charge of affairs, as elegantly dressed as a diplomat, led them along rows of crammed clothing racks, which he treated like a delegation from below stairs.

Apple tried on jeans and windcheaters, sweaters and shirts. Their labels, he slyly noted, were Canadian. Chosen items would receive an ageing, the man said languidly.

That was the last call. On their way back Agnes

talked of Walter Brent's wives, who had each won a
divorce settlement in excess of ten million dollars. Apple was wondering what approach he would try next to
get information on the caper.

Midnight, when they arrived, Agnes set about making supper while Marie took over as talker, in French.
After spending five minutes on Brent's close friends,
she started on tapestries. When a pause came, Apple
said, "You're both good and thorough. I appreciate
that."

"We haven't really got down to it yet, dear. In the
morning, after you've spent the night on our couch, we
start packing the information in hard, as well as showing you videos of all the people concerned. Believe me,
you'll know everything worth knowing about Walter
Brent by the time you have your next meeting with Mr.
Watkin."

"Yes, just before I fly off into the blue," Apple said. Sly
again, he spoke as though he knew what he was talking
about.

"That's right, dear. How nice for you."

"You're familiar with my destination, of course."

Marie shrugged. "I have been there."

Pleased with his cleverness, Apple said a casual, "You
know and I know, so there's no need to talk of it."

"Precisely. Now back to tapestries."

Five minutes later Apple said, "It's possible I know
more than you ladies do about this caper I'm going on."

"Dear, we know nothing of it whatever. But nothing."

"Oh."

"It's usually better that way."

"Well . . ."

"So please don't tell me anything."

"Okay."

"It's enough to know that you'll be in sunny Cannes."

"Oh?"

"It shouldn't be too busy with tourists, in spite of all those extra people there for the bibliophile convention."

"No?"

Apple was still digesting the news, still enjoying its aftertaste, when Agnes came in with a tray and asked Marie, "Did you remember to tell One when he first arrived about Cannes and the convention, as per Mr. Watkin's instructions?"

"One of us must have. He knows."

"Good."

"He knows everything, I bet," Marie said. "But he's not giving any of it away, as befits a real professional operative."

She and Agnes gazed admiringly at Apple, who basked.

The public library was within walking distance, for which Apple was thankful. He'd had a long day's wait into evening. His buttocks had become as numb with sitting as his mind had with all the information it had needed to absorb, none of it quirky enough to be interesting.

As he strode through the tedious streets, under a light rain, Apple was further uplifted by embracing that inside four or five hours he would be heading for the Côte d'Azur's balmy glamour.

Preferring to think of it blasély, Apple dissembled by laying his cheer's source both at the door of Agnes and Marie's hospitality, just ended, and at his own stoic decency at not mentioning how badly he had slept on their six-foot couch.

After he had seen Angus Watkin, Apple was to go home. While he settled the flat to survive his absence, also telephoning the United Kingdom Philological Institute's recording machine to leave a message, he would receive a caller bearing gifts: boots, hair-piece, clothing, documents in the name of Thomas Wainwright, sundries, plane ticket from London to Nice, all in one suitcase of Canadian manufacture. The hairpiece he was to put on when in the taxi between Nice and Cannes.

"The driver," he had said, "is one of ours."

"No, he isn't," Agnes had said. "Which means he'll notice this curious act and no doubt tell it around. Can't hurt."

It was typical of Angus Watkin, Apple mused as he went through the library entrance, that these mundane details of the mission would be passed on by others. Himself, he was above such matters, a theologian declining to pass the plate.

Inside, a broad aisle led to the desk, with on either hand rows of free-standing banks of bookshelves. Browsers were outnumbered by the desk's array of staff.

Apple went into a lane between banks. At the end he made a U-turn into the next lane, whereupon he saw his Control. Angus Watkin was at the far end, beyond the aisle, standing in the pose of reading.

Retracing his steps, Apple crossed the aisle and arrived on the other side of the shelves from Watkin. Pleased with himself, having always liked this bit when seeing it on television, he moved volumes until he was looking through a space at his chief. He said, "Good evening, sir."

The space Angus Watkin promptly filled up with his book. Appearing around the corner, he said, "Brilliant."

"Sir?"

"If you weren't warned against these inventions of the fictioneers, when your mind was being cleansed of the unworkable, surely you would be guided by common sense."

Knowing he couldn't be sent on a mission without being made to feel small, to be set clear that his importance was limited, Apple mused that probably this had been in his mind when he had done the book-shifting routine—to give God Watkin his opportunity, get that done with in order for the business at hand to move on.

"Sir?" Apple said again, eyes acting worried, mouth not showing how smart he felt.

"In this particular case," Angus Watkin said, "a third-party observer, if not a crowd, is presented with the picture of a person apparently talking to himself. Eminently watchable and decidedly memorable."

Allowing his mouth a taste of freedom, Apple said, "Hadn't thought of that."

I know you hadn't, so don't pretend you had, Watkin's mouth seemed to imply in its faint, wry twist. *Why do you think I stood here in the first place?*

Apple straightened his face with a sighed, "All right."

"I beg your pardon?" Watkin said. "Never mind. I suggest we pursue the matter of this meeting."

"Good idea, sir."

"Thank you, Porter. Please attend."

With him using Porter rather than One, the theologian, stating that he didn't even need to know the plate-passer's name, last-worded on who owned the cat and who was merely a claw on its paw.

"You are going to Cannes as a bibliophile," Angus Watkin said. "A private collector. A buyer in search of a seller."

Apple thought he had better not say that a seller in this field was called a bibliopole. He asked, "I'm after a rare book, sir?"

"A manuscript, which from here on we will term the Property. It has a good chance of being in Cannes this week, at the annual convention of collectors and dealers and middlemen, thieves and forgers and liars, all eccentric to some degree."

"So the one who has the Property is a dealer."

"That is unknown," Angus Watkin said. "But certainly he will be hoping to sell. Neither he nor the Property are being talked about outside the peculiar enclosed world of bibliomania, and not much inside it. People are wary of referring to a situation with such a lethal potential."

Because he knew it was expected of him, Apple asked with a suggestion of concern, "Lethal, sir?"

"The Property, to use the vernacular, is dynamite. Many governments would go to extremes to get hold of it. Already one man has lost his life under mysterious circumstances. Perhaps two have."

"Obviously, then, these governments can't simply buy it, for some reason."

"Buy it they would, gladly, and pay any price, if they could corner the proprietor. Naturally, he is afraid that, instead of money, he'll get a bullet. Also he might not be the legitimate owner, or be legitimate himself. With extreme caution, therefore, he will be looking for a private buyer."

Apple said, "Enter Walter Brent."

Watkin said, "Well done."

"Thank you."

"Although this manuscript is not the type of work he would normally find inviting, which change his eccentricity should explain away, Brent suits perfectly. Both for us and the seller. Brent is incredibly wealthy, and, unusual in the rich, is known to be generous. He is honest. He is discreet. In short, he is the perfect buyer."

"Then it should be plain sailing, sir."

Angus Watkin said, "Only if the seller—let us call him Owner—is aware of Walter Brent's existence, which isn't at all sure, since not many people are outside the trade, and signs say Owner could be an outsider."

Judiciously Apple said, "Awkward."

"We have done our best. Word has been put out that Brent will be in Cannes, to avoid publicity using a different name and in disguise—including elevator shoes to make him look taller. It is to be hoped that Owner will pick up this information and seek you out, Porter, though meanwhile you will be doing your best to find *him.*"

"Indeed I will, sir."

"Preferably before the competition."

Ignoring the implied insult, and not wanting to ask if the competition formed a danger to Walter Brent/Agent One, Apple asked, "How complete is our dossier on Owner?"

Almost it seemed with pleasure, Angus Watkin said, "There is no dossier. There is nothing. Owner could be male or female, young or old, of any nationality—though possibly Austrian—a clever person or a fool."

Apple murmured, "Handy."

"All we know for sure is what happened recently, in

Vienna. A respected book dealer, an expert on the Property's subject and a graphologist, telephoned a friend in great excitement. He had just finished examining a manuscript, which he pronounced genuine. While still making the call, he died, apparently of a heart attack, which admittedly does fit with his excitation, itself understandable. The friend told his wife and others what he had heard—including that the dealer had offered to go to the approaching Cannes convention for the manuscript's owner, as middleman seller— excluding details on the owner himself. Later that day the friend was killed in a hit-and-run accident."

After slow nods Apple asked, "The competition?"

Angus Watkin gave that twitch of the shoulders which for him was an expressive shrug. "Impossible to tell from here. Despite the fictioneers, the hit-and-run arrangement is rarely brought off successfully." Unless arranged by Angus Watkin, a following twitch suggested. "Be that as it may, you now understand the circumstances."

"I do, sir. A difficult and dangerous mission."

"A mission slightly problematical and with a thin element of risk, yes."

Before Watkin had finished saying this, the expected reducer, Apple had started telling him briskly that all he needed now was to know what manner of manuscript it was for which he would be putting his life in jeopardy.

He ended, "Is the Property vital to some country's national security, sir?"

Unperturbed by having his reducer slimmed, Angus Watkin said, "Not in the least, Porter. Face is involved, not security. Prestige, if you will. Perhaps even honour."

"Whose honour?"

"Ours. The Property is an attack on possibly the most famous Englishman of all time: Sherlock Holmes."

Apple's mouth felt weak. "An attack?" he said. "But dismissable, surely. Deridable."

"Not with ease. It was written, purportedly, by the author himself, Sir Arthur Conan Doyle."

"Impossible," Apple blustered before recovering fast due to being unused to bluster. He said, "It is, of course, a forgery. Of course it is."

"The late book dealer, as I stated, was a graphologist," Angus Watkin said, "as well as one of the world's many many Holmesians—which, we must presume, is why Owner contacted him. The book dealer concluded that the hundred-page handwritten document is Sir Arthur's work."

Apple pointed out, "Some experts will authenticate anything so long as they're in for a commission. It happens all the time with paintings."

"True, Porter, and I agree that the Property is more likely than not a forgery. However, if it's good enough to split opinion, it might just as well be real."

Glumly: "I see that."

"Also it is known that Conan Doyle came to dislike his detective. He killed him off once, but public and editorial demand forced him to bring him back to life. After that he hated Holmes thoroughly."

"How is it that the manuscript didn't come to light earlier, if it's genuine?"

"That is nicely explained," Angus Watkin said. "Doyle wrote it toward the end of his life, when he was involved in spiritualism. He told friends of an important Holmes manuscript which he had hidden and which he wanted published posthumously. The hiding place he would divulge through a medium when he had crossed the Rubicon, he said. Need I add that the message was never received?"

"No," Apple said.

"We are to assume that someone, probably Owner, stumbled on the hiding place by happenstance. Then he set about establishing if he had found rubbish or gold."

"But how is the manuscript an attack on Holmes, sir?"

"Doyle tells about the real person from whom he took his fictional character," Angus Watkin said. "In addition to being an awful man on several different scores, the original was totally addicted to cocaine, of which he had a constant supply through his brother, with whom he lived. The brother was a doctor. A decent man, people came to him with problems that were personal as well as medical. The addict interfered, generally with disastrous results."

"But they gave Doyle ideas for stories?" Apple asked.

"Just so. They, he admits, are feeble on logic. He scorns them. He despised anyone who thought they were good and proves that Professor Moriarty had more brains than Sherlock Holmes. There's more, it seems, but that is enough in itself."

"I should think so."

Watkin said, "Over all, the whole concept of the detective is besmirched. It would spell his end if the Property were to be published. Obviously, therefore, it has to be acquired so it can be suppressed, destroyed."

With fervour Apple said, "Obviously." He was impressed by the gravity of his mission. He felt important.

"And that is all I have to tell you," Angus Watkin said, curt in finality.

"There is one other thing, sir."

"Time is getting short, Porter."

"The thing is this: How much am I allowed to offer? How much can I spend?"

His Control stared at him bleakly. "Just get the Property, man. One way or another—get it."

"Yes, sir."

"Good-bye," Angus Watkin said, coming forward, going past.

Apple turned with him. He asked, "What'll happen, by the way, if the manuscript turns out to be genuine, not forged?"

Watkin tossed back, "Then its destruction will have to be all the more thorough."

Feeling not important but suddenly uncomfortable, Apple mused as he watched Watkin's figure recede, *Destroy a valuable piece of literature merely in the name of national prestige?* His mouth felt weak again.

TWO

Apple awoke to the chatter of birds, sunshine and the sound of a woman singing. This happy trinity raised him into a sit in bed, smiling as he gazed around at the old-fashioned room complete with matrimonial bedstead and a wardrobe big enough to accommodate a lover.

The birds were beyond the window, undraped, through which sunshine beamed like devotion past annoyance; the woman was somewhere beyond the door.

Just in time, before he could sour, Apple reminded himself that he had promised interimly not to think of the possible destruction of literary gems. He was going to enjoy his caper in the sun.

A knock sounded on the door and a key rattled into its lock. Apple called out in French, "Please enter." The door was open and the maid singing her way in with a breakfast tray before Apple realised he was naked from the neck up. He yanked the sheet over his head.

The maid stopped singing. In a subdued voice she bade the guest a good morning and hoped for him a robust appetite. Apple gave appropriate replies from behind the sheet, immobile except for one gesturing hand. The maid left in a continuing silence.

Clever, Apple decided as he got out of bed. That was what it had been of him to do the hiding bit, thereby adding another star to Walter Brent's reputation as an eccentric along with further evidence of the guest being that same Walter Brent.

The fact that Apple was registered here at the Mérimée as Thomas Wainwright he ignored. After stretching, he brought Bernard out of the wardrobe.

So dubbed by Apple because when empty it looked like either the head of a dead saint or a drunken dog, the hair-piece was almost as efficient as a ski-mask in respect of hiding features. When pulled on and patted into snug place, as now, the spread of gingery curls showed only eyes, nose, lips and small sections of cheek.

Bernard wasn't going to interfere with the fine Gallic cuisine he intended sampling here in Cannes, Apple noted gladly as he began on breakfast. Croissant in one hand, coffee in the other, he stood eating at the window, bold in pajamas.

The Mérimée was one of those intimate hotels that hide some five or six blocks back from the sea, not so much shy as aloof. Tall and narrow, determinedly baroque, it had a small surround of garden rich in bougainvillea and oleander, well off in white-painted furniture, poor in contrived charm.

By touching his brow on the glass, Apple could see three floors below to the gateway. It was still being guarded by a policeman with an assault rifle, colleague of the one last night who had requested politely, "Your papers, please, sir."

As the woman at the desk had been on the verge of falling asleep, Apple hadn't asked about the police watch. He intended doing it soonest.

However, when Apple entered the cramped lobby an hour later, wearing jeans, windcheater and Bernard, its reception desk was deserted. Giving a Quebec click of the tongue, he left and headed briskly for the Carlton to advertise his presence.

During Cannes's most famous convention, the spring Film Festival, those international cinema magazines which normally publish by the week or month put out an edition locally every day. In them, attending nobodies can free of charge announce their attendance: *John Dough, Ind. Prod., looking for properties, Hotel Martinez.*

This week the same obtained with an English-language, Berlin-based, Dutch-owned quarterly devoted to books and manuscripts, letters and autographs.

Striding through the neat streets of shops which welcomed all but the economy tourist, Apple soon reached the Croisette, Cannes's elegant promenade. Above carpetesque sward, palm-tree fronds wafted sexily in the sea breeze and large hotels smiled down affectionately on moneyed strollers and Mercedes taxicabs.

Prominent stood the Carlton. It was like a castle that had been frosted. Going in, Apple's thoughts were on the legions of movie stars who had trod this same path, before the Festival had become mainly a trading post, grading from art to mart.

The lobby, with its upcurving staircase in a rear corner, was noisy and crowded. No one paid any heed to Apple as he crossed to a table where a girl was giving away copies of *Scrivenings.* The temporary office, she said, was in room 217.

It was full of similar girls, Apple found on going upstairs. They, chatting in German about parties and receptions and hemlines, took so little notice of him that out of pique, one he failed to recognise, he was led to assert himself in filling out the form he was casually handed.

Rendered creative thus, he hit on the idea which he wrote out as, "Thomas Wainwright of Canada, selling early detective fiction mss, Hotel Mérimée."

Neat, Apple self-congratulated as he left the room. As neat as his announcement idea itself. The item said it all without saying a thing.

Downstairs Apple went into the bar. Although it, too, was crowded, he managed to find a duet table by the French windows, which were open to the terrace, whose tables were also packed. Sitting, slumped low, he kept his attention on his copy of *Scrivenings* until the waiter had returned with his request for typical local elevenses, which turned out to be English tea and an American doughnut.

From his skip through the slim, pictureless periodical, Apple garnered nothing. The names were unknown to him and none of the items were as open to interpretation as his own.

Looking around, Apple was pleased to register that he was not going unobserved. More than one person switched eyes away on them being reached by Apple's roving gaze. Some of these persons were obvious eccentrics, which meant they stood a good chance of being conventioneers.

One matron wore a hat formed like a boar's head on a plate, complete to the mouthed lemon. A man, swarthy and middle-aged and ugly, still looked cool despite his overcoat with a fur collar. Two men wore yellow rain slickers, another was asleep, a youngish woman had on sufficient necklaces to set up in business and two couples were using mutes' hand-language while carrying on a normal conversation.

A short stout Oriental in a panama hat was drawing on a meerschaum pipe which gave out no smoke even though its bowl was glowing red; on Apple's second look he saw that patently the light came from a tiny battery-operated bulb.

Cheered by the insanity of that, Apple bit lustily into his doughnut. He was swallowing the last bite when he became aware of a stare, one with the subtlety of a searchlight.

Slanting his face downward so he could peer unseen through Bernard's canopy of curls, Apple looked beyond two tables and pinpointed the starer, who was a new arrival.

Thirty, in tourist plumage, the man of ordinary appearance was staring the look of enquiry, an expression which matched the way Apple began to feel: Where have I seen him before?

Apple itched in the armpits with nervousness. It was almost inevitable, he knew, that on a caper someday, somewhere, he would come across an acquaintance. Was this man with the familiar features a Bloomsbury neighbour, a clerk from the United Kingdom Philological Institute, a mechanic who'd had the honour of servicing Ethel? There were hundreds of possibilities.

Surely there had to be a standard procedure for agents to use in situations such as this, which couldn't be all that rare, Apple fretted, briefly, before shifting his mind away on recalling having had the procedure taught to him at Damian House. What he couldn't recall were details.

Apple's every muscle clenched at the next move. Face clearing to a smile, the man rose suddenly, which caused his table to jerk, which caused a glass to fall off it and land with a crash, which caused the assembly to pay instant attention and reduce all talk.

The man was plainly heard when he said in British

English, beginning to circle intervening tables, "Of course. Now I get it. I would've known you anywhere."

Apple, eyes sad, rose to a crouch. He was unaware of shaking his head and whispering, "No."

The man said, "That wig had me fooled for a minute. What's the idea?"

"No," Apple whispered, himself going forward, his intention being to effect some manner of containment. He was seeing his caper dissolve on the first day.

"So how are you, Wally?" the man asked. He put out his hand.

Apple grasped it. "What?"

"Fancy seeing you in Cannes, Wally old man."

"Ah yes. To be sure."

In a lower tone the man asked, "How'm I doing, One?"

Weakly Apple said, "Fine." He remembered now. They had been underlings together once on a mission, bystanders with orders to jostle a KGB courier, who, in the event, went in the opposite direction.

The agent said, "God Watkin thought a little help wouldn't hurt, since I had to come and give you a bit of info anyway."

Recovering with deep breaths, Apple said, "You could've let me know you were going to do this."

"I'm told you're not a hotshot at acting," the Brit said. "This way you looked truly disturbed."

Even though knowing that the opinion on his skill as an actor was wildly wrong, Apple nodded in forgiveness. The assembly, for the main part, had lost interest, he noted. This was the famous Carlton Bar, after all, where uncelebrated friends were wont to enter by different doors so they could greet one another loudly, with extra decibels on the giving of names.

Recovered to the point where he could feel jealous of how well the Brit had done that table-knocking/glass-breaking/attention-getting routine, Apple asked coolly, "What's the info?"

The agent said, "French Intelligence is in on the deal. You will have seen the guard on your hotel, front and back."

"True, I will."

"Ostensibly it's because the building's under the protection of the National Heritage Board, and terrorists might try to blast it, for publicity."

"What's the real reason?"

"To keep various secret service oppositions, the Competition, from eliminating Walter Brent when he's at rest."

Apple strolled east along the Croisette's outer side, where, a short drop below, beach ran along beside grey sea. He was not alone. English residents walked their poodles and natives walked their whippets.

While telling himself he was no more concerned about the danger than he was about the possible destruction of literature, Apple felt sure in regard to another matter that he needn't worry, that the agent would tip well for the mess in addition to paying for the broken glass.

That over, Apple stopped to look back. It wasn't the first time he had done so since leaving the Carlton, and he was intrigued to see that he had been right last time, probably, about having a pair of tails.

One, a white Rolls-Royce with dark windows, was creeping along near the kerb. The other was a man in a panama hat who could be that Oriental with the weird pipe.

Apple didn't know if they were goodies or baddies, but did recognise them as singles, not a team, because they were both on the same side of the roadway, just as he knew that they could have been alerted by the agent's "Wally."

It was going to be confusing, Apple realised, distinguishing between those who wanted to eliminate him as a buyer, those who genuinely wished to purchase early detective fiction, and the one who hopefully wanted to contact him with a view to selling him the Property.

The panama-hatted man had come closer before halting, as the Rolls had already done. Seeing that he was indeed the Oriental, Apple christened him Wiley, and mused: Progress.

Moving on, he decided that in spite of the possibility of his tails being Competition, he would give them every opportunity to make an approach. What was a spot of danger, after all? It was all part of the espionage business.

Apple's head was sweating. Walking directly in the sun, being encased inside Bernard, from the jawline upward he had become hot and slimy. It was like blushing in a Turkish bath. Or so Apple supposed. He had never owned the nerve to go in a Turkish bath.

Without quite admitting to himself that this was happening, scratching at itchy flesh slyly through the curls with alternating hands, Apple moved to the kerb. When traffic eased, he went across to the strip of super-immaculate lawn dividing the twin roadways, where the palm trees gave shade.

No, Apple pretended as he walked alone between the two streams of cars, the grass was not the plastic he had suspected, but real. It was sensible to check these things out.

His head cooled. Soon he was able to begin wondering if walking on the grass was illegal, which was in his mind still when a car eased alongside from behind. Its driver was wearing a uniform.

Next, from his vision's edge, Apple established the car's flying-lady mascot and general glitter. He doubted if the local police patrolled in Rolls-Royces. The driver, of course, was a chauffeur.

Turning his head sharply and looking down, Apple met the gaze of the tail-car's sole passenger, though through the glass darkly. The man frowning up, as ugly as sin's reputation yet with none of its promise, had been in the bar, wearer of a fur-collared overcoat. Aged in the region of sixty, he had black hair greased flat to go with villain features and looked like a disgruntled falcon.

Instinctively Apple turned away. The other roadway clear, he stepped into it and strode across to the far side. Vaguely unnerved by Falcon's ugliness and glower, he kept going into an off-street.

Like a hunted animal in search of cover, Apple mused in light derision, which didn't make him stop. In any case, at roughly the same time he was acknowledging what a good idea it was to change tack in order to ascertain whether or not he had tails. Falcon, after all, could have been about to complain about the grass-crushing.

Having left behind the stretch of hotels on the front, Apple was coming into a purely residential section. He didn't look back, for doing so would have been too noticeable in the hereabouts desertion.

After several fast-covered blocks, Apple came into a

large open space. It was a parklet-cum-recreation area.
Near at hand old men were playing *boule*, the Conti-
nental adult version of marbles. The metal balls were
big enough for tennis, the grit pitches as unpretentious
as the small-coin wagers.

Separating pitches from road was a tree-shaded
fence, where Apple leaned. Another minute and he
had semi-forgotten tails. He was involved. It wasn't the
game itself, but the players. He was fascinated by the
way they contorted their bodies after a throw, bending,
teetering, flailing an arm, standing on one leg. He
wasn't conscious of his own body making the same
moves in miniature.

When Apple returned to himself it was because of
footsteps. They were approaching from behind. He
stayed in his lean on elbows, tense, wondering if he was
the goal and if so would it be Falcon or Wiley.

The girl asked, "Mind if I join you?"

Still not moving, except for his head, Apple relaxed as
he examined the blonde, who was tall and willowy, long
of straight hair and striking of tanned face, age perhaps
twenty-five. She wore peasant skirt and blouse, the latter being generous with a view of cleavage. Her language was North American English.

Apple said something casual to the effect of it being a
free country. "I guess."

Hitching up the shoulder-strap of her bag, the blonde
said, moving closer, "Actually, Mr. Brent, I've followed
you from the Croisette."

"Mr. Who?"

"Walter Brent, Mr. Brent. Please call me Susan."

Apple said lightly, "You know, Susan, this is the second time today someone's taken me for your Brent
character. Who is he anyway?"

"Please don't play games with me," the girl said, bland. "I'm serious."

"And what, Susan, are you serious about?"

"My job. My profession. I'm a journalist, presently with the Toronto *Globe and Mail.*"

Apple nodded. "Some people claim to be reporters because they think it gives them the right to be nosy."

Reaching to her bag, the blonde said, "If you like, I'll show you my credentials."

If she was Competition, Apple knew, her papers would be good enough to fool all but an expert, let alone an underling. He said, "I'll take your word for it. But you're barking up the wrong tree."

"I don't think so, Mr. Brent."

"My name is Thomas Wainwright. If you like, I'll show you *my* credentials."

"Never mind," the girl said, continuing bland. "I guess a man in your position could buy the best in any department."

"Position?"

"Wealth."

"Have you come to put the bite on me, Susan?" Apple asked while telling himself if he straightened from his low lean he would have an even better view into that cleavage.

"No, Mr. Brent. I'm not a beggar. I've come to ask you for an interview."

"I doubt if the *Globe and Mail* readers would be interested in an obscure book dealer who's trying to sell detective-fiction manuscripts."

Susan didn't blink or unbland. "Okay," she said. "Let's pretend your name's whatever you claim it is and that all this hair is for real. I'd still like to talk to you."

Apple stood fully erect. "You're talking to me already. And why don't you call me Tom?"

"Right on, Tom. And what I meant was with a tape recorder. Mine's in my room at the hotel. We can walk there in less than five minutes."

Gazing down at the view: "Mmm?"

"My hotel room, Tom," Susan said. "You're not scared of me, are you?"

Apple collected himself. He looked from ripe flesh to cool eyes and stopped musing that here he was, involved in a caper on the exotic Riviera, complete with sunshine and palm trees, shapely blondes and veteran gamblers. He felt uncomfortable.

Susan offered cigarettes. Apple shook his head, and while doing so managing to scan behind. There being no hint either of Wiley or Falcon didn't make him feel any better. His emotions were mixed, uneasy in one another's company. He was sympathetic, guilty, wary, hopeful.

The girl could be everything she claimed, a hard-working journalist. If so, his impersonation could cause her private hurt of professional harm. She could be Competition and therefore lethal. Although she was unlikely to be Owner, she could be a go-between.

Blowing out smoke forcefully after lighting a cigarette, Susan said, blandness gone, "Please, Mr. Brent. I mean Tom. I need a scoop badly. It's my last chance. I'm on the point of losing my job. I implore you as a fellow Canuck to give me a break."

With one final, farewell glance at the view, Apple took a step backwards. Continuing to reverse, he said, "Tell you what. Meet me this evening. Seven o'clock. In front of the railroad station. Okay?"

He turned and began to stride off, hearing, "I'll be there, Tom. Thanks."

Apple spent the next hour walking. He stayed among people for safety while getting to know the town and self-assuring that he was making himself available approachwise as Walter Brent the buyer.

Several times he thought he glimpsed Wiley in the rear distance, though there were Japanese tourists aplenty, and Falcon could have been in one of the unrare white Rolls-Royces whispering around the insidious streets like tedious arguments that follow the claim that the rich are unhappy. Apple enjoyed his stroll. He kept in the shade.

It was when both sides of the boulevard he had come onto were bathed in sunshine that Apple realised he was hungry. On either hand were restaurants with outside dining areas, these topped by scalloped awnings, edged by privet hedges in tubs. He went to the nearest.

The table he chose allowed him to have his back to the wall. Disappointingly, the menu presented to him was the size of a postcard. Handing it back, he asked what was the chef's special today. Same as every day, the small chirpy waiter told him: "Pizza Garibaldi." With fortitude Apple realised that the restaurant he had picked was not French but Italian. He ordered a pizza.

As the waiter turned away, his place was taken by someone not much taller, though of twice the girth. Apple awarded Wiley ten points for his unseen approach, saying, "I don't want to buy anything, thank you."

"I am not a street peddler," the Oriental said in Oxford English, a polite smile on the face of smooth plumpness. "It intrigues me, however, that you should take me for one." He lowered the hand that had been touching his hat brim in a form of salutation.

Pleased to realise he was annoyed at feeling let down that the man lacked the standard Eastern accent, Apple said, "Then how can I help you, sir?"

"In no way. I merely wish to give you something."

"Oh yes?"

It was a copy of *Scrivenings*, produced with a flourish from behind his back by the stout man, who explained, "Yours. You left it in the Carlton."

"So I did."

"I followed you with it from there but lost you, being a stranger to Cannes. And then I happened to see you sitting here, Mr. . . . ?"

"I'm Thomas Wainwright. And you are?"

Wiley's answer sounded like a retort in an argument. He added, "Originally from Kyoto, I have lived in Europe for many years. I am a collector of rare and antique writings."

"I'm something similar," Apple said. Wondering if it were normal for strangers to immediately give their professions and to put themselves out to return free periodicals, he rose slightly off his seat to shake hands.

"I thought you might be in the same field," Wiley said. From a pocket of his fawn linen jacket he brought out the pipe, which he held near his chest, as pipe-smokers do, as though it were a sign proclaiming the bearer to be a solid fellow.

Apple said, "By way of thanks for the magazine, and because we're colleagues, may I offer you a glass of wine?"

"That is most cordial of you, Mr. Wainwright. I accept."

"You could even have a slice of my Pizza Garibaldi, if you were so inclined."

"The drink will suffice, thank you."

Within minutes a half bottle of table wine brought, they were chatting like commuter acquaintances, and Apple was feeling drab. He had concluded that A, the Oriental transplant was probably irrelevant to the caper, and B, that it was a shame how in the spy game people who weren't relevant, no matter how fine they might be, made you feel drab.

Wiley, hat still in place (bald, Apple guessed), was talking about his pipe. "The bulb gives a tiny light and a smidgen of warmth, so I have that to go with the oral and manual gratification. I lack only the smoke."

"Which is dangerous to the health."

"That I don't care about. But burning embers can be extremely destructive to manuscripts. I had to quit smoking."

Apple stated, "You're a dedicated man."

Nodding: "More than that. It's a passion with me, literature. Perhaps an obsession. The financial side of it concerns me the least."

"What d'you think of this, then?" Apple asked, tapping *Scrivenings*. He thought the true bibliophile's opinion would be useful to own, as well as any other information he could gather.

"There are better journals," Wiley said.

He went on to name names, which Apple only part heard, being taken with a curious aspect of the magazine. Its corners were neat. Distinctly he remembered bending one of them by accident when he had begun to read in the bar. This was not his copy of *Scrivenings*.

Apple looked up. He said, "Yes," which he hoped was right. Had Wiley, he wondered, concluded that *he* was irrelevant? Or was he caperwise straight, a nice guy who had procured a clean copy of the magazine to return to the mislayer?

Wiley said, "But you must know all the periodicals, of course, Mr. Wainwright."

"Of course, of course."

"And *Books Today?* Do you subscribe?"

Apple said an absentminded "Avidly."

"Interesting," the Oriental said. He took a sniff of his wine, tapped the pipe stem against his bottom teeth. "There is no such journal as *Books Today.*"

The atmosphere had changed, although Wiley himself seemed no different, mouth still formed in its polite smile, eyes playing miser with his emotions.

"Just so," Apple said. It gave a dram of satisfaction, like trying on a hat you fancied but thought looked too big and finding out you were right.

"Which means what, Mr. Wainwright?"

In timely fashion the waiter appeared with a Garibaldi. As he put it down the Oriental got up, saying, "I will leave you to your lunch. But we will meet again."

"We will?"

"Undoubtedly. We may even be able to do business. I like your caution. Good day to you. I hope you enjoy your Pizza Moriarti."

Apple watched the stout man go with mixed feelings. He told himself he would have to stop trying to guess goodie or baddie with everyone he came across on this brief mission. It wouldn't get him anywhere in the short run.

Apple also told himself as he lingered through the delicious pizza that it had been smart of him, turning down the page corner like that.

Meal over, bill paid and committed to memory to be

put on his expenses sheet, Apple went inside the restaurant and through to the back. There were one or two loiterers on the street he didn't care for the look of. Passing washrooms, he went into the kitchen. Staff glared until Apple began to speak. He used Italian. After having charged his Garibaldi with having been superb, plus dropping that its name came from the fact that it brought ingredients from all parts of Italy together as one entity, he saluted and left. That he did so by the back door produced no protests.

The first vacant taxi that appeared Apple stopped. During the ride he found peace from a niggle by admitting that perhaps his overbending of the page corner had not been intentional after all.

The policeman at Hotel Mérimée's gate looked bored. He ignored Apple when he strode past. Inside, his thoughts on a Mediterranean siesta, Apple was stopped by the owner from behind her desk.

A small woman with white hair rising like an upside-down wedding cake, she handed over a rolled periodical: "This was brought for you, *monsieur.*"

Apple had no surprise on recognising a copy of *Scrivenings.* Attached was a calling card, on which a message was scrawled. Denver Campbell of Edinburgh was leaving the magazine, forgotten by Mr. Wainwright in the Carlton Bar.

The first thing Apple did after his post-siesta shower was put Bernard on. The first thing he did when dry was dial Denver Campbell, getting no answer. The first thing he did after dressing was examine the new *Scrivenings.* It had a buckled corner.

Humming as he sat in an armchair to give the magazine a thorough reading, Apple let himself know distantly that despite the nonsense by the Brit agent in the bar, he had managed to get things moving.

From his read Apple learned that some letters from Stalin were to be included in Thursday's auction, that in London a Rudolph Hess autograph had just changed hands for a large sum of money, and that tonight's supper-reception at the Hotel Lincoln was open to all legitimate dealers.

He went downstairs. No, the proprietress said, neither she nor anyone else had been on duty when the periodical was delivered but did know it came by one of the scooter messenger services.

"It had a name on it?" Apple asked.

"No, *monsieur*. It smelled of exhaust fumes."

"You should have been a spy."

"I was one. For the Underground during the war, along with about ten thousand others."

Apple didn't begin to feel special again until, strolling by a roundabout route, he came to the railway station. Before the glass face lay an expansive frontage, on which people were numerously standing or milling, waiting or in transit, mumbling good-byes or calling hellos.

Apple's usual ability to see over heads was reduced, part because he sagged so as to make himself less noticeable, part because of Bernard's dangle of curls. However, he had no worries about missing Susan when he started to drift slowly through the crowd. She was due any minute now.

At crowd's edge there erupted a minor commotion. Coming on shrewd, Apple ignored it, for he didn't want to spoil his concentration on the section by section scan he was making of the gathering. The commotion faded.

Not finding Susan, Apple became less diffident about

being seen. He started to walk tall, inviting notice. There was still no Susan. Apple went through the crowd dissectingly as well as around its edges. Susan stayed absent.

When she was thirty minutes late Apple thought she might not be coming. What bothered him was that he didn't know whether to be annoyed at being stood up, relieved at being taken off the hook, worried about something maybe having happened to the girl.

He continued to circulate through the thinning crowd until eight o'clock. Although he hadn't given up entirely, convinced that she would show up the moment he left, he went into the station to find a telephone.

With the folding door closed against noise and his claustrophobia on hold, Apple dialled the calling-card's number. A deep voice with a Scottish thistle in it said, "Denver Campbell here."

"I'm Thomas Wainright. You kindly returned my *Scrivenings*, Mr. Campbell."

"Nice of me, I thought."

"Which is why I'm calling. To thank you. Also to learn how you knew where to find me."

"Simple," Denver Campbell said. "I had noticed this tall hairy type enter the Carlton lobby from upstairs. A nice lassie at reception told me no such type was registered as a guest. But upstairs is the office of that same periodical."

"Got it," Apple said. "Neatly done, Mr. Campbell."

"Elementary, Mr. Wainwright."

"Er—elementary?"

"Quite. A simple matter."

A knock sounded on the door's glass. Looking around, Apple saw a man. He was hefty and unhappy, beef stretching tight a seaman's sweater, a grimace of impatience worsening his wrestler features. He would have had a crew-cut if his hair had been able to stand up.

After signalling that he would soon be finished, Apple turned away. He asked into the receiver, "Did they also tell you in the office, while giving you my address and name, what's in the item I'll have in tomorrow's edition?"

"I did happen to notice those while the girls were showing me the form you filled in."

Jocular: "There ain't no privacy."

"That which is free, Mr. Wainwright, is free." The name was pronounced heavily. "Public domain and all that."

"Perhaps you'd be interested in my detective-fiction manuscripts. Do you collect?"

"Buy and sell," Denver Campbell said. "Yes, detective fiction does interest me, actually."

Apple looked around again at another knock, this one no louder than a short burst of thunder right overhead. The Scot asked, "What was that?"

Unhappier, Bullybeef snarled in French, "How long you going to be, son of a whore?"

In the same language Apple told him nicely, "Just one more little minute."

Campbell asked, "What did you say?"

Apple told him, "I have a minor problem here."

Denver Campbell: "Not, it seems, with the French language."

Bullybeef snarled another insult and used a head-sized fist to create more thunder. "Come on out of there."

"One minute," Apple said, holding up one finger,

which, he was surprised and concerned to see, was
sticking out from the middle of the bunch.

Denver Campbell said, "I'll be in touch. Good-bye."
The line died.

Apple put down the receiver. Smiling like a patient
who refuses to give in to his infirmity, he went outside.
He managed not to limp.

At once, shoulders up like cats' backs, Bullybeef began a tirade whose language had been born in the worst
slums of Marseilles. He came forward as implacably as a
dread appointment, and Apple backed off showing his
palms for peace. He questioned if this anger could be
real.

"Insult me, would you, you bastard?" Bullybeef said.
He nodded as though to encourage confirmation.

"Wouldn't dream of such a thing, friend."

"Now it's calling me friend. It's piling one insult on
top of another."

"Perhaps I'm mistaken after all," Apple said anxiously, only semi-acting. Baddie or innocent, Bullybeef
seemed bent on doing physical damage. "I was sure
we'd met before."

"Watch what you're saying, germ."

"Don't I look familiar?"

"No, you long-legged pimp," Bullybeef said. He
made a sideways swipe at the peacemaker hands, clat-
tering them together painfully.

"Think," Apple said. "Paris last week. The Moulin
Rouge. You were dancing with that beautiful young
actress. I was with the Interior Minister's wife. She in-
troduced us. You really don't remember?"

For a second in Bullybeef's tiny eyes appeared a light.
It could have been the spark of longing or a glimmer of
regret. Next, it was gone and he looked unhappier than

ever. He spat that he hated the Interior Minister, who was a pig, as were all his friends.

"Then it was in the asylum I saw you," Apple said recklessly, growing tired both of the harassment and of his Chamberlaining. "You idiot."

Massive though he was, Bullybeef had the speed of a nervous flyweight. "Abuse a poor honest hard-working docker, would you?" he growled—before throwing the lightning right that landed on Apple's chin.

Only the fact of his unusual height, so easy to misjudge, saved Apple from the blow's full force. Instead of falling flat he staggered backwards.

Bullybeef followed. Snarling that nobody could insult him and live to tell the tale, he threw another righthander. It missed, but he was fast with a long left.

Apple was still trying for complete balance. The blow got him on his cheek and he went into another stagger. This time he fell. After crashing against a vending machine he slumped down into a sit.

Bullybeef wasn't finished. Ignoring the dozen or so observers who were protesting with cries and fierce gasps while reversing discreetly, he came on with outthrust jaw and evil eye. He snarled, "It's going to get it now."

Apple tried to get up. He couldn't.

That Bullybeef had never heard of the Marquis of Queensbury became clear as, faintly, he broke step in his approach. He was going to kick.

Too dazed for competent coordination, Apple was still struggling like someone crawling upside-down when the kick started. Its goal was his head.

The stranger appeared as opportunely as a comic-strip hero. He zapped into view on Apple's left, swoop-

ing, and with an accurate grab took hold of Bullybeef's
foot, which he threw high before letting go.

Bullybeef went drunkenly backwards. He fell over
onto his back, but, professionally, wrenched himself on
in the standard bum-over-brain twist. He rolled.

The stranger turned. He was forty, fair, athletic,
tanned, of good-looking if jowly face, wearing a green
velvet sports jacket and a Tyrolean hat of the same
colour. Reaching down a hand, he said cheerfully:

"You all right? That was close. Sorry I don't speak
French. But I dare say you get the pitch." His language
was German with a Berlin accent.

Taking the hand, Apple pulled himself up. He hesitated, not knowing how to play this. Gaining time, he
pointed. Tyrol turned to see Bullybeef getting up with
determination. Over his shoulder the rescuer said, "Excuse me. I'll just deal with this fellow." He strode off.

Apple did a fade.

Although twilight was only a pretty promise yet, an
expression in the evening's eye, lights shone every-
where in the streets of central Cannes. The air had the
balminess that occurs mostly in cheating memories.

He could have enjoyed the ambience as he walked,
Apple mused sulkily, if he had been able to stop dwelling on that scene at the station, which made him feel
guilty.

Bullybeef could easily be Competition, Apple knew,
and, more likely than not, was. There were fewer point-
ers to the ulterior with the other man, but he certainly
could have been attempting to establish a cozy relation-
ship via his rescue routine. He could also be a true
Samaritan, one who ought to have been thanked pro-
fusely for his decency and courage.

The man was probably disgusted, Apple mused, pink inside Bernard. Next time he saw a similar situation he would maybe walk away, leave the victim to his fate. So could be the victim gets rolled, Apple pictured. He goes home penniless and battered. His wife accuses him of being drunk. They have this terrible fight. Their child runs out distraught. She doesn't see the speeding car until—

"Straight ahead, *monsieur.*"

Apple stopped. "What?" he said, staring at the Ambassador to the Court of St. James's, who then took clearer form as a headwaiter. "Oh yes. Thank you."

Crossing the Hotel Lincoln's lobby, Apple passed into a large salon. It was packed and noisy, with a layer of tobacco smoke hovering like a convention of haloes between heads and low ceiling. Everyone had either a glass or a plate or both.

Out of the crowd emerged a panama hat. Hoping with an amusement which wasn't quite pure that he wouldn't get paranoid about hats, Apple smiled strongly as Wiley came up and during their handshake.

The Oriental said a theatrical, "We meet again, Mr. Wainwright." He touched his hat brim.

"Why, so we do."

"A most interesting gathering we have here. I'm tempted to write a little monograph on the looks of one hundred and forty different varieties of bibliophile— buyers, sellers and middlemen."

Taking the cue, Apple said, "Myself, I'm a seller. The who-done-it stuff."

"I came to look for friends. One's Donan Coil, if you know who I mean."

"Sorry."

Wiley said, "But I mustn't keep you from your supper, Mr. Wainwright. Over in that corner you'll find the buffet. It's Indonesian food."

Half an hour later, having eaten while thinking of something else, though not of victims of assault, Apple began to circulate. He carried a glass of Perrier water disguised by lemon and ice as a gin and tonic.

There were, he found, several familiar faces. He exchanged nods and murmurs, boldly chatted to the boar's head woman who now had a hat like a galleon, noted the sly looks he was getting, ignored a man who said, "Good evening, Mr. Brent."

Since Apple was unconsciously moving in a stoop (that layer of smoke had to be avoided), he heard clearly when behind him a woman said:

"I couldn't agree more, Mr. Campbell."

Going on, Apple didn't look back until he had rounded another person, one whom he could use for cover. What he saw to match the deep voice of the Scot was a thin pale man of about fifty with thin pale hair and a prominent nose. He wore a three-piece tweed with most of the nap worn off, as if it had awakened to the fact that Cannes was hot. Giving his attention to the woman, he looked as though at any minute now he was going to repeat, "Elementary."

Apple would have stayed on, watching, if he hadn't realised that he was being observed himself, by the cover person. As Apple's stance made it appear that he was trying to see into his own breast pocket, the man watched him with a smile ready, in case it was all a riot.

Apple straightened and sidled away. It was on account of being as tall as he could get that he saw Falcon.

The ugly man, still in his fur-collared coat, was coming this way. He wasn't a jot any the less sinister without the white Rolls-Royce around him.

Sinking at the knees, Apple went quickly off to the side. It would be best to avoid Falcon, who could only be trouble, because with a face like that he couldn't possibly be anything else and certainly not Owner. Apple told himself this in confidence.

Over the following hour he continued to circulate. During his wander he noted several girls with pretty faces, kept on the move when one of these dropped her handkerchief, told the pair of local reporters who buttonholed him that he was a Swede who collected Caruso letters, asked three people, with no success, if they could please point out to him the celebrated Walter Brent.

Apple had decided to leave—crowd thinning, Falcon getting harder to avoid—when he came face to face with Tyrol, whom he had failed to spot, he defended, because the hat wasn't being worn. Apple gave one of his long Ahs.

"Hello there, Mr. Wainwright," the tanned man said in guttural English.

"Well, hello."

"As you hear, I know your name and nationality. I took the trouble of asking."

"Er—who?"

"A lady in a strange hat," the man said.

Apple said quickly, "Many, many thanks for your help at the station. The reason I didn't stay to thank you then was because I had to meet someone urgently."

"My name is Carl Schmidt, and that is not true. You had no one to meet."

"I beg your pardon."

Calm, Tyrol said, "I know the real reason you left like a shot out of a gun."

Apple was almost blushing. "You do?"

"Of course. You've knocked around the world, obviously, as I have myself. You thought it was that old business where the rescuer and victim have a drink together after the attack, and the rescuer either asks for a loan or pretends to have lost his wallet while fighting. It's operated in all countries, partners of Tough and Hero against Victim."

It was also, Apple recalled now, one of the methods in espionage of getting on fast, close terms with a mark. Known as the Two-Card Trick, the reason it hadn't been in Apple's immediate recall was because at Damian House he had played Tough in a practice session and had been knocked down by Victim.

While protesting that he had most decidedly not thought Tyrol part of a criminal team, that he had indeed had an urgent appointment, Apple was musing: could still be Competition. Two-Card Trick fails so Tyrol makes another stab with an exposé of it, allaying suspicion. Neat.

"Thank you for your confidence in me," Tyrol said. "But let us go and have a drink together. I promise to do the paying and to not ask for a loan."

And be led into a trap, maybe? Apple thought. He said, becoming agitated after a glance at his watch, "It kills me but I've got to decline. At least for now. How awful. You'll think me the most ungrateful slob of all time. But I have this urgent meeting."

"Another?"

"Same one," Apple said, backing off. He darted forward to give Tyrol's hand a hasty shake, started reversing again, patted his watch because he could think of no way to explain why the meeting was so urgent. It hurt him that the tanned man looked genuinely disappointed, even wounded.

At a distance, just within earshot, Apple called out, "Give me a ring. I'm at the Mérimée. We'll get together for that drink." Turning, he hurried off.

Out on the street, the sky above black, Apple was putting his handkerchief away from having given those small exposed parts of his face a wipe, when the girl came up beside him with, "How corny can you get."

To go with the Eastern-seaboard American accent was an American face—small nose, agile eyes, strong jaw and wide mouth, dry skin, all arranged to form a regulation prettiness. Her dark hair, short, was untidy by design. The dress she had moving around her was loose and gaudy.

"Young lady," Apple said, "I have no idea what you're talking about."

The girl perked, eyes widening. "Hey, you speak my language. In fact, you're an American."

"Canadian. The name's Thomas Wainwright. What was that about corn?"

"Dropping something near a person to make contact. Women have been doing it with hankies and fans and stuff for untold centuries, but I didn't think men ever did it. Hello. The name's Tilda."

"Hello. I must've been copying that girl inside. She did the drop bit. Maybe it was you, Tilda."

"I was inside but I didn't drop anything," the girl said. "And if you were in there, how does it happen I didn't see you? You're tall enough."

Apple said he didn't know. "Nor, come to think of it, do I know what you meant about me, in respect of the dropped."

He noted now, as the girl raised her hand, that she

was holding a folded piece of paper. "This," she said. "You mean you dropped it by accident?"

Supposing it must have come out of his pocket along with the handkerchief, Apple said hammily, "Absolutely not. I wouldn't dream of not trying to pick up a pretty girl."

"Hey, that's real gallant of you, Thomas Wainwright. You're a cute one."

"So're you, Tilda. Not the type to be in there with all those old and young fogies."

"Part of the job. I'm working as private secretary to a dealer, based in New York. This is my first time in Europe, and I think it's terrific."

Apple, realising they were walking together, moving with other nighttime strollers, asked, "What does your dealer deal in particularly? First editions?"

"All kindsa stuff," Tilda said. "Here he's looking for something special."

"That right?"

"Take your paper, why don't you."

After he had put the folded sheet in his pocket, Apple said, "Something special, eh?"

Tilda said, "I don't want to talk shop."

"What do you want to do?"

"Go for a swim. Coming?"

While Tilda went on to talk of the beach three blocks away, Apple was trying not to listen as he told himself all this was too lush to be true; and, naturally, she wasn't headed for a lighted pool but the dark beach. He preferred to hear that it was all perfectly natural, and nothing would suit him better than being alone on a deserted beach with a pretty girl.

What Apple did listen to was the advice that he should work at finding out if Tilda was kosher. Mean-

while, to give himself time to think method, he slowed
his walk.

He was outdone by the girl. She stopped. Putting her
hands on her hips, which persisted in a stroll sway, she
asked, "How can I be sure about you?"

"I'm not with you, Tilda."

"Corny the dropped-whatever routine may be, and
accidental it could be, the fact remains that it worked.
Here we are."

"I told you I did it on purpose."

"Seriously," Tilda said. "You could have motives."

"Apart from more corn, boy-meets-girl?" Apple said.
"Give me a for-instance."

"Well, as my boss says, this racket is loaded with spies
and finks and phonies."

"He said that?"

Tilda nodded. "If not in those exact words."

"I'll know if I have motives or not if you tell me the
name of your boss. Or what he's looking for. Could be
he's a rival of mine."

"Don't think I'll tell you anything. I think I'll keep
the crazy book world out of it altogether."

"Suits me," Apple said as though he meant it.

Tilda brought her hands together in a clap. "Well, it's
me for a swim, Thomas."

"I don't have my swimsuit. Nor have you."

"I've got it on."

"Sure you have."

With a swoop Tilda bent down and up, lifting high
the hem of her dress. Underneath, on a twinkling body,
she wore a crimson bikini.

A passing woman gasped, a passing driver pomped
his horn, and Apple, furious at feeling embarrassed,
fought back by being businesslike. Knowing that one

way to get to a subject's true self was via startlement, he
said in an awed tone:

"But you've got nothing on at all."

With a light shriek the girl dropped her dress. She
groped beneath it and panted laughter around, "Boy,
you really had me there for a sec."

"Sorry," Apple said with nothing proved. "I'll walk
you to the sea. You'll need guarding from the Hound of
the Baskervilles."

"Whoever he might be," Tilda said. As they walked
on she talked of her excitement at being here on the
fabled Riviera. That she ended with a yelled, "Race
you!"

Apple stopped, being that a line of traffic had cut him
off from Tilda, who was racing across the Croisette. To
fill the wait he went into his pocket to see if what he had
dropped at the Hotel Lincoln had been of consequence. He brought out the paper. Even before he
started on unfolding, he realised it wasn't his property.

"Come on," Tilda shouted from the other side.
"What're you waiting for?"

Apple looked up from examining the photocopy. He
called out that he had to go. "Emergency."

"Oh no."

"Why don't we meet here tomorrow. At noon, say.
Swim and lunch. Okay?"

The girl shrugged, wagged her head, measured a metre with her hands and called, "It's a date, Thomas.
Twelve noon."

Apple turned away. He headed swiftly for strong
lighting in order to have a better look at this photocopied page of manuscript whose longhand several
times formed the name of the world's greatest fictional
detective.

THREE

Apple was awake and respectably ready when the knock came, having left word downstairs last night that he wanted his breakfast at ten o'clock; which wasn't especially true, since he would be hungry long before that; what he did want was the pleasure of saying it. He lay neatly flat under the sheet with Bernard in place.

On his call to enter the maid came in, unsinging. She had farmgirl jotted down all over her like names on a plaster cast. Her eyes, cautious, accepted the hairy head but shied from what Apple had given no thought to: the other end. As usual when he wasn't in his own long bed, his feet were sticking out into space and wearing their Rover Boy warmers.

The maid got her tray onto the table, albeit bumpingly, while keeping her back not turned toward Apple's feet. She left with a low, *"Bon appétit."*

Thanking her coolly, Apple sat up. He drew his feet under the sheet. A gift from an aunt, he always used the warmers if he didn't arrange to forget to pack them because a promise was a promise and his late aunt had been the poorest one in the family.

Once his work to remove his warmers under the sheet was done, Apple's attention went to the breakfast tray. He noted two things. First, on it there was an envelope. Second, the envelope was smoking.

Leaping out of bed, Apple went across for a close

look. The milk, he saw, had slopped from its jug, no doubt during the maid's bumping, wetting mainly the envelope's face, from which area vapor was rising. Deep sniffs told that an acid was involved.

While Apple knew that chemical-impregnated paper was rarely lethal, true it was that the one who handled it, activating same with moisture (sweat), would become ill enough for a stay in hospital. Ill enough to be out of the running in a mission.

With pincered fingers Apple took the envelop by a corner, carried it into the bathroom and flushed it into history. He telephoned down to reception. The letter had been delivered by messenger, the woman said.

After snapping his fingers at the danger for the rightness of it, congratulating himself on his convincing performance as the peculiar Walter Brent, and nodding at his conviction that Aunt Regina had always been his favourite, always, Apple began breakfast.

He was still eating when the telephone rang. The caller identified himself as Denver Campbell. He said, "How about if we get together this morning for a little chat, Mr. Wainwright."

"Suits me fine, Mr. Campbell. Shall we say the Carlton Bar at eleven?"

"We shall indeed. Until then."

"Wait a minute," Apple said, waxing crafty. "How will I recognize you?" Officially, he had never seen the man.

"No problem about that. I know what you look like and I'll be there early. If you wish, however, I could carry a copy of *Scrivenings* in one hand, a tulip in the other and be gazing east, the kind of thing the spies do."

"I believe we'll manage without the frills, Mr. Campbell. Until eleven."

As he put the receiver down, Apple mused that the Scotsman couldn't be ruled out in connexion with the photocopy. Last night he had been at the reception along with Wiley, Tyrol, Falcon and the headgear lover Hattie, as well as many unknowns, including the waiters. Any one of them could have been responsible for getting the paper into his pocket.

Last night here Apple had passed an enjoyable spylike hour examining the page of manuscript. Although its written matter made little sense, being out of context, it did establish the author as Sir Arthur Conan Doyle or his impersonator.

One edge of the page had been ripped off untidily. This basic gambit for purposes of identification showed, Apple recognised, that at some future point the reverse-pickpocket wanted to be able to do a matching of edge with page, saying in effect, "I was the one who passed it to you and I have the whole manuscript."

Apple rubbed mental hands over a fact of which he hadn't been certain before: Owner was in Cannes. He was here passing out samples and looking for a deal. Possibly he had wangled photocopied pages into the possession of everyone whom he considered to be a star buyer.

The starriest buyer was Walter Brent, Apple assured himself loyally. So all Agent One needed to do was stay alive, healthy and available while continuing his worthy pose as the eccentric billionaire.

And what, Apple thought on, would be more realistic and in character than for multi-wed Walter Brent to put his collector affairs aside in order to go swimming and lunching with an attractive girl?

Apple was forced to admit, however, just when he had started to feel nicely cynical, that his date wouldn't be a complete steal of time from the caper. Tilda, whose return of the photocopy could have been a really sharp reverse-dip, at the same time establishing contact, might be involved up to her cute little nose.

Humming, Apple went to have a bath.

Like an airport's VIP lounge when the imminent closure of its free bar is announced, the Carlton lobby was bustling. People were there with purpose. They had come in to circle once or twice as part of their morning constitutional along the Croisette. They were avoiding plainclothes security men, who looked like pickpockets. They veered close to checkers-in not so much to eye their bags' labels as to be seen smiling at them sardonically. They waited for out-of-town friends by not watching the staircase, down which they knew would come those same friends, who were staying at one-fork pensions.

Apple, who had collected a copy of *Scrivenings*, stood at one side of the lobby to check on his item. It was there and all correct—and, he realised, could have been responsible for bringing that acid letter.

As he looked up from having folded the periodical, Apple saw the girl called Susan. Or thought he did. The glimpse of sun-lover face and blond hair over by the entrance was brief as a slow blink. Susan or her lookalike had been headed for the outdoors.

Apple went that way, at a surge, using one arm to open a path ahead and holding the other up above the crowd like a deep-water wader. People tutted. Apple accepted the disapproval gladly as part of a caper's hardship.

He reached the sighting point, went on, reached the main door, went out. In scanning around with care, stopped, he saw no signs of either Susan or a girl of similar type.

Clicking his tongue in dismissal, Apple went back inside. He told himself: philosophically, that she must have found a better scoop; professionally, that she couldn't be involved in the mission because she would have made contact; masochistically, that she had every right to stand people up if she felt like it; disdainfully, that the only good reporter was one who had grown up into a journalist.

Denver Campbell was present, sitting alone near where he himself had been yesterday, Apple saw as he strolled into the bar. He kept going in that direction. Almost, he gestured when the Scotsman looked around and saw him. He went on by the table, doubling back on hearing, "Here I am, Mr. Wainwright."

One minute later they were sitting side by side with preliminaries over. Ten minutes later, after talk of weather and Wordsworth, prices and Poe, a waiter brought the order, which enabled Apple to say, apropos the charge-slip, "I ought to get a photocopy of that."

The pale man with a dark voice, thin in his worn tweed suit, looked at him acutely. "Photocopy, did you say?"

"In jest, yes."

"I'm afraid I miss the joke."

Apple explained that if they both wanted the charge-slip for their expense accounts, it would have to be duplicated. "But it's not big enough to bother with, of course, and I don't have an expense account anyway."

"Nor do I, Mr. Wainwright," Denver Campbell said.

He covered the slip with a banknote. "I imagine that your means, like my own, are private."

"That's so, Mr. Campbell."

"Then here's to unneeded photocopies."

"Here's to 'em."

The Scot lifted his whiskey, Apple his tea. When they had both tasted, the while eyeing one another like prospective in-laws, Denver Campbell said:

"Before we go any further, I have a wee something for you." He produced a small silver tube. "A friend gave me this cigar. I'm anxious to get an opinion on it. Perhaps you would be kind enough to oblige me, Mr. Wainwright."

Apple translated nuances and found, *If you are Walter Brent, you'll know about cigars, and, because I returned your lost magazine, you can't very well refuse me.*

Which would have been fine with Apple except for the decision in London that Agent One would say, in his Brent role, that he had given up smoking, since there was insufficient time to feed him cigar information.

However, Apple saw, if Denver Campbell was Owner, a distinct possibility, using any excuse whatever to get out of this test would itself be a result, a convincer that Wainwright was not the billionaire in disguise. Apple knew he would have to go through with it.

He accepted the tube. After unscrewing its top with an expert's faint tolerant smile, he did an upending so that the wrapped cigar slid onto the palm of his hand, which he then dithered as though it were a highly sensitive weighing device.

Face up, he told the ceiling a soft nasal, "Not too bad, not too bad."

Denver Campbell watched closely, of which Apple was aware but indirectly. He was keeping his gaze off the thin man, as befitted a connoisseur who was intent on exercising his judicative faculties.

The cigar's wrapping was a flimsy of wood. This Apple took off with insouciance, the way a man might blow froth from his beer. He tossed it into the ashtray airily.

Denver Campbell seemed to nod.

Apple put the cigar under his nose at moustache level. Slowly he moved it back and forth from end to end, the while taking short sniffs through alternating nostrils. Lastly, changing the angle to upright, he smelled first the open end, then the bite.

Judgement Apple pronounced by giving the far wall one heavy, slow nod with his right eye almost closed. This could be interpreted, he knew, as anything from a respectful Super to a tired Vile.

It was when Apple began to pat pockets that the Scotsman broke his silence. Deep voice held in rein, he asked a quiet, merciless, "Are you not going to roll it beside your ear, Mr. Wainwright?"

Taking his time, Apple swung his head to look at the thin man. He looked at him as though they had met only once before, years ago, when Campbell had beaten him to the last seat on the last plane out of that grim place.

The Scot licked his pale lips. Apple said in a dull, Watkin voice, "Dryness or lack of same, Mr. Campbell, has been tested for already, as you may have noticed."

"Oh? When?"

Borrowing another from Angus Watkin, deafness: "Rolling a cigar beside the ear or anywhere else, *squeezing* it, is not only gauche but brutal."

"Well . . ."

"Let us move on."

Seeing Apple again patting pockets, the Scot said, "You may use my clipper, if you wish, Mr. Wainwright, should you have forgotten your own."

"Decent of you," Apple said. He had been patting his pockets because, as before, he didn't know what to do next, and he wouldn't recognise a cigar-clipper if he saw one. "Very decent. I know how people are about their clippers."

"I'm not the possessive type, fortunately."

"Myself, I gave them up. I use match or toothpick."

Denver Campbell brought out a box of matches. "Please be my guest, Mr. Wainwright."

Apple took his time about chavelling to a point with his thumbnail the end of a matchstick, which he then, delicately careful, hands at eye level, used to pierce the cigar's bite. He used it a second time to light up.

Praying that he would neither get smoke in his eyes nor cough, Apple took tentative puffs. "Mmmm," he gave out, back to nasal. "Mmmmm."

"Mmmmm, Mr. Wainwright?"

"There's an amusing little fore-bouquet."

The Scot was intent. "Ah."

"Quite light. Floating. On wings. It hints of the Canary Islands."

"Well now."

Apple puffed some more. "Yes indeed," he said from behind a cloud. "The sub-aroma from the inner leaf has a certain voluptuous hedonism."

"Really?"

"It's fiercely independent. One would even be tempted to say arrogant."

"I see."

Gaining confidence from not coughing or getting his eyes stung, Apple blew out a long luxurious stream of smoke. He felt successful. He felt powerful. He wished the girls from the typing pool could see him now.

Cigar held at a distance and looked at, Apple said after several clops of his mouth, "At the heart of the matter is an intriguing savour, a green light and dark. Part of it is trying to be genteel, show off its breeding, another part is being a trifle bellicose."

Denver Campbell, still intent, performed slow nods before saying, "May I interrupt with a question, Mr. Wainwright?"

Punctured by the knowledge that he now had to deliver an opinion on what might be a wonderful product as easily as it could be a piece of rubbish, Apple came down from euphoria with a slap.

He said a dead, "By all means."

The Scotsman asked measuredly, "What's become of your Canadian accent?"

Apple paused. To keep his mouth from making odd shapes he put the cigar into it fast, this while still realising with shock that so absorbed had he been in what he was saying that he had used his natural speech-form to say it.

Denver Campbell purred, "Mmm?"

Apple answered gibberish with the cigar in place, creating a hollow mumble like a convict eating at hymn time. Campbell said, "I beg your pardon, Mr. Wainwright?"

Apple removed the cigar. Inspired, cool as rain, his phony accent back in place, he said, "My education in smoking took place in London clubs. I wouldn't dream of speaking anything but clubland English when discussing cigars. In fact, I do it instinctively."

"Curious," the Scot said, thoughtful.

As though catching sight of someone across the room, Apple changed his expression and waved. In a bustle, beginning to rise, he said, "There's that guy who wants to sell me an odd manuscript. Must go. Thanks for the tea. Let's do this again real soon, huh?"

Apple was on his feet now. Before he could move away Denver Campbell shot up a hand and caught him by the sleeve. He asked, cold, "What, please, is your verdict on the cigar?" His eyes flicked to where it lay in the ashtray.

Equally cold, though with a hint of condescension: "That I can't give you, Mr. Campbell, I'm afraid. For two reasons. One, a cigar has to be smoked at least halfway through before it divulges all its secrets."

Following a baleful lull: "And two?"

Apple said, "My taste is off because for some reason or another I wasn't offered, along with my cigar, the traditional glass of brandy." He eased his sleeve free of the grip. "Good day to you, Mr. Campbell."

Leaving by the French windows, Apple came onto the terrace. Its tables were full, with here and there a familiar face, yet not one that Apple thought might show a satisfying response if he mentioned photocopies to its owner.

This ploy he would continue, Apple had decided, even though he felt that Denver Campbell was probably in possession of the Property. Otherwise, why would he go to such trouble to establish Thomas Wainwright as Walter Brent?

To avoid dwelling on whether or not such establishment had happened, his act with the cigar convincing,

Apple whistled out of tune to aggravate his mind as he moved on and made his way to the terrace front.

There, half a dozen steps took him down to the pavement. He turned left. Across the twin roads farther along was where he would be meeting Tilda, in a quarter hour.

To pass time, Apple began to circle the block, strolling. He felt fine. He was ready for anything. Subtle dangers he was alert to on account of that envelope and under his clothes he wore a swimsuit.

Apple was thinking about the envelope again when, having almost completed the block circuit, he drew level with a rack of picture postcards. It was outside a souvenir shop. Stopping, putting a fingertip on his bottom teeth, Apple thought over what had just occurred to him. He could, after all, send a postcard to Monico.

His dog, an Ibizan hound who lodged during the week at a farm near the Porter country cottage, would be indifferent to a card that came in the ordinary way, rendered overkill smellwise by multihandling, Apple reckoned. If, however, the card arrived for Monico sealed in an envelope, so bearing only the scent of his friend . . .

Moving closer, Apple started to look at the pictures. But at once he took pause. Wasn't this a bit ridiculous, he questioned, sending postcards to a dog? His nonlogical side questioned right back, Why not? He answered by pointing out that Monico couldn't read. In that case, he countered, there wouldn't be the tiresome problem of filling up that space with words.

The resolver was time. With a glance at his watch, Apple strode on toward the Croisette. He halted on the corner, whereupon he saw his date, Tilda, who, over by the seawall, saw him at the same moment. They both waved.

Apple, telling himself he had two minutes in hand, decided to go back and buy a postcard, because if he didn't do it immediately, he never would, he'd be sensible instead of ridiculous, which would be right and proper and extremely drab.

The signal Apple intended sending to Tilda he kept back when his view of her became obscured by a car slowing down there. He turned and marched.

Coming to a stop by the rack, he bent to look at its postcards. Their pictures, bright and cheery, were mostly views of the town. Apple reached for a shot of the public library, changed his mind, told himself to find something with trees, began to turn the rack in jerks. There were pictures with trees, but they weren't too interesting.

Apple stopped the rack. He dithered over an arty shot of a single palm, but it showed only the burst of fronds at the top, nothing of the lower part, which would have the greater interest for Monico. He wondered if he was losing his mind.

Apple's watch beeped. With a wrench, he forced his body away from the rack. He returned at a run to the Croisette and had crossed the first roadway before noting that Tilda was no longer there.

Nor was she below on the beach, he saw on reaching the low wall. He looked beyond, to the sea a hundred metres away, where it trickled in with its tranquil Mediterranean lap-lap. Tilda was not among the bathers. Turning, Apple scanned the Croisette in all directions. No Tilda.

During the twenty minutes he waited, Apple took turns at blaming himself for having gone away, which must have had a permanent look, and blaming the girl for not hanging around to see what happened next. He left.

Similarly, during the half hour he spent buying a picture postcard (basket of puppies) and an envelope and a stamp, writing his dog's name on the card and addressing the envelope to Farmer Galling, Apple took turns at seeing the stand-up as normal and, since it was a repeat of the case with reporter Susan, as sinister.

He found a mailbox on a street corner. Telling himself firmly that he was doing the right thing, that puppies were definitely preferable to a kitten with a stupid ball of wool, Apple slid his envelope into the mailbox slot.

About to walk on, he saw that someone was in his way. He looked down at Wiley, who said, "We meet yet again, Mr. Wainwright."

"Not by accident."

"It's not?"

Apple said, "I've been tailing you."

The Oriental blinked up from under the brim of his panama. "You have?"

"Only joking."

"Oh, that's too bad, Mr. Wainwright. It would explain the sensation of being followed that I've been having."

Apple nodded. He had been having the same sensation, he was now able to admit, with company, which lessened the suggestion of paranoia. In any case, that trailing-finger feeling across the shoulders had been intermittent, meaning either that he was being looked at because of his unusual height, or the hound was a quality operative who knew better than to continually keep his eyes on the hare.

"Perhaps it's merely my imagination," Wiley said

with an encouraging nod. "One can be influenced in these matters by unfamiliar surroundings."

"You're bound to draw attention with that pipe of yours," Apple said. "Maybe you should carry a photocopy of it instead. For you alone to look at."

Unresponding: "Your sense of humour, Mr. Wainwright, is somewhat surrealistic."

"There's absolutely nothing wrong with photocopies, in my opinion."

"Good."

"Maybe you feel differently."

"No," Wiley said, giving the subject a farewell. He began to talk of last night's reception at the Hotel Lincoln, where by sheer luck he had run into an old acquaintance called Hums. "Sheer luck," he said. "Hums."

"That's nice," Apple said, brisk as frost. "But I really must be off."

Another minute and he was striding along the shopper-busy street. When he stopped again, it was by the ideal vantage place, an angled storefront that allowed him to look back the way he had come through its window reflection.

Taking his time, Apple was able to pick out four men who were dawdling and who could have been hounds. They could also have been waiting for nonshow dates, settling on which person to mug, or following each other, Apple knew. Whatever, he concluded that a bout of slip-giving was in order.

Wondering what was so special about Wiley's acquaintance Sheer-luck Hums, Apple stepped away from the store and at a funereal pace went on. He let everyone get in his way. He lazily window-shopped. He loitered to lend a helping gaze to a man painting a door.

He was yawning as he showed his profile in turning a corner.

Snapping alive once out of sight, Apple ran. He went swiftly along the street and then several others, turning finally into one that was a dead end. Some of the businesses on either side were restaurants.

In the one Apple entered at random, wanting to be among the unseen, every table was vacant. Hating to be the sole diner as well as knowing that emptiness meant indifferent food at best, he would have backed quietly out except that a waiter appeared. Even then Apple might have made an excuse to leave had it not been for the relief and gratitude showing in the man's dark face, in his welcoming bow, and in the way he resettled his turban.

It was as much the only other diners to arrive, a grim-faced couple, as the man lounging across the street, that sent Apple through to the rear when he had paid for his meal. He went into the kitchen. Not stopping, he circled toward the back door while telling the chef, in Hindi, that the curry had been excellent. He lied.

Vaguely pleased behind the guilt (it was warming to be false), Apple stepped out into a backyard. It led to an alley. This brought him onto a street where traffic flowed. After a glance behind to check that he wasn't being tailed, he waved at an approaching taxi. It stopped.

Settling back on the seat as the taxi moved off, Apple called out the name of his hotel, calling on account of being separated from the front by an expanse of glass. The driver raised a hand.

With his thoughts wandering—from wouldn't Monico be surprised to the fact that Wiley was out as Owner to the best way of making a curry to the value of white lies—Apple took no notice of direction for a while. When he did, seeing they were going the wrong way, he assumed the driver to be pulling the old routine of making a ride last as long as possible, if his fare was an obvious nonlocal.

But when, presently, Apple saw that they were headed out of town, the last chance to turn for the Mérimée gone, he knew with a trill up his spine that he was the victim of a neat abduction. Or there was a mistake.

Leaning forward, Apple rapped on the glass. The driver, who had a shaven head and a neck as thick as a waist, made no effort to look around. There was no mistake.

Not wasting time on the glass divider, which would be bullet-proof strong, Apple tried first one door-handle and then the other. Both were locked—by a central system, he guessed.

He grabbed the window-handle. Hardly had he got it circling before it came away in his hand. Same thing happened at the other side.

Apple looked outside. They were in a suburb, housing with spots of commerce. The road had traffic ahead and behind, the pavements had ample pedestrians.

Getting attention might be the solution, Apple thought. With a handle in either hand he began to pound on the near-side window.

The clatter brought around the driver's head, showing heavy features set in the glee of solitary confinement. But all Baldy could do in containment of the noise was increase that frown, it seemed.

While musing that what the abductors should have

arranged was a method of filling the back with a knock-out gas, Apple clattered on.

Passers-by looked. Some grinned at the maniac, others shook their heads as though they thought they were being offered something; same gave warning frowns, others looked quickly away.

At a set of traffic lights the taxi stopped. As it did, Apple heard music blast into being. The driver had his radio going and his window down, treating the vicinity to a generous helping of heavy rock.

Apple continued his clatter. But no matter how he changed the pattern of his beat, it still sounded as if he were supplying percussion to the music, playing drummer.

Those pedestrians who didn't veer away from the yammer and clatter snapped their fingers at him or nodded in encouragement. Two girls in punk gear crowded their green hair to the window, where they gyrated like ballerinas on vacation until the taxi moved on.

"Sure," Apple said, tossing the handles aside.

He lay on his back on the seat, next move already in mind. Although he knew that a Mercedes was a particularly solid car, he knew also that door-catches were never infallible, especially if the vehicle was in motion.

Being long, Apple was able to rest his shoulders on one door, his feet on the other, and still have his knees bent. He applied pressure. It did occur to him that if the door behind him flew open instead of the other, he might be in trouble, but what waited for him at his destination could, he was aware, be worse. He pressed on.

Nothing happened.

They were now in an outer suburb, wholly residential, with only a scattering of walkers. The taxi's speed was being dictated by other vehicles, but that, Apple realised, wouldn't continue. Soon they would be in open country, where speed would force him to stay inside even if he did manage to create an escape route.

About to try higher, glass instead of upholstered door, Apple recalled that rear windows were the weakest of all. Furthermore, the glass was stressed, like the windshield, to break outwards, and in bits rather than shards.

Apple changed position. With his shoulders pressed on the front seat, bracing with his hands on the floor, he raised both feet high. His sent them out together in a powerful double-kick. His shoes slammed against the rear window.

It broke.

The sound was like a bag of cement bursting from a fall, on a pile of bottles. Cubes of glass shot off in all directions, mainly outwards. The driver shouted. The taxi lurched.

In smooth haste Apple moved over the seat and began to get through the window space. He went crabwise, aware of spectators in other cars and of the fact that the taxi was slowing.

It had reached a conveniently languid pace by the time Apple was lying out on the back. He let himself slide off, in reverse, landing on his feet and pulling forward into a short, stammering run.

Drawing into the kerb, the taxi halted, which seemed to indicate that its driver wasn't ready to give up, abandon the abduction. Apple didn't relish the idea of tangling with a heavy, though this he managed to impute to his having just eaten a large meal.

The taxicab door snapped open wide and Baldy came

partway out to look back with a red glare. Bluffing, Apple ran forward. He waved his fists, he bellowed with rage. After hesitating for a sickening moment, the driver went back inside and slammed the door. He drove off.

Apple came to a reluctant-seeming halt. Fists he lowered to hips, a stance of belligerence which was only part acted. Already he was beginning to forget his lack of relish a moment ago. When, taxi gone from sight, he turned to walk the other way, he adopted a slight swagger.

To settle his dithery nerves, Apple walked back to town. In any case, he was in no hurry. For safety and shade he chose quiet streets. They were so quiet he was yawning by the time he got to his hotel.

Three people had telephoned to ask for him and had left their numbers, the proprietress said. The latter piece of information she delivered as though it were a coup she had pulled off at some risk, thereby rendering the disaster of his nonpresence less severe.

Apple thanked her gravely. He could not, he accepted, very well object when she moved merely a token one metre away while he used the desk telephone, the receiver of which she had handed to him firmly.

The first call put him in touch with Tyrol, who asked, "How about that drink, Mr. Wainwright?"

Apple said he had some photocopying to do. "I'll ring you again later." Tyrol said nothing, a meaningful silence to which Apple didn't know the meaning. He said, "So long for now."

The other two calls were connected with his *Scrivenings* item. Both parties, Frenchmen, wanted to buy early detective fiction and responded in no way to a pointed reference to photocopies.

Thanking the owner again by giving her a look of relief, Apple left the lobby. Upstairs, in his room, he didn't see the girl until he had closed the door behind him.

She was lying facedown on the bed. She wore nothing apart from mascara and a chain around one ankle. Her breathing was deep, her hair was a cap of dark curls, her side-turned face was pertly attractive, her eyes were closed, her bottom had dimples.

So much noise did Apple make in trying to get quietly out, when, after a careful contemplation of the naked body to see if it was known to him, he decided he must be in the wrong room, that the girl stirred and came awake.

Rolling over, she looked at him in friendly fashion and sat up. She made no attempt to cover her nakedness. In French she asked, "What's all the noise for?"

"Sorry about that."

"Who are you anyway?"

"I'm afraid this is my room," Apple said with a bow of apology, admitting what he had known all along.

The girl glanced around with dark quick eyes. She said, "I believe you're right."

"Thank you. My name's Tom."

"Mimi. Hello. You're very hairy, aren't you?"

"Yes. You're very shapely, aren't you?"

"Yes. Would you pass me my cigarettes, please. I like hairy men."

"Of course. I like shapely women."

Mimi grinned. "You're very funny and your French is quite hilarious."

Her things were piled on the breakfast table. Willingly Apple played attendant. He was enjoying the piquancy of the bodyscape with its pear-shaped breasts and smiling navel, plus the strong possibility that caperwise his visitor was not an innocent.

Having declined a cigarette, as well as a sample from the brandy flask in her bag, Apple stood nearby happily while Mimi smoked and chattered.

She was a salesgirl in a real classy dress shop, she said, down here from Paris for a little break, get some sea air, have a good time. She told about her last lover and her cat and the bitchy concierge where she lived.

If she was phony, in reality an espionage operative, Apple mused, then she was brilliant at it. But he reminded himself that everything she said could be one hundred percent true—and she could still be an agent, one of the faceless variety. Her speciality would be sexual entrapment.

Prompted by Mimi on her third cigarette, Apple talked about Thomas Wainwright. He was strongly aware that he sounded, at least to his own ears, less than convincing. This, he decided on instant reflection, must be something he was doing on purpose, subconsciously, to see if the girl's attitude became less warm.

It did not. It became, in fact, even warmer. She took back the conversational ball and Apple was treated to a course on dress sales talk, with bust-weaving gestures.

Stubbing out her fourth cigarette, Mimi asked, "Did you come back here to have a nap?"

"Well . . ."

"Because you may. Just get undressed and lie down. If I'm taking up too much room—say so, and I'll leave."

Apple was tempted. However, the given being of paler value than the attained, he was, despite the lush body, able to resist, for the time being.

"Later that would be wonderful," he said. "But right at this moment, unfortunately, I have to go see someone. About a photocopy."

"At once?"

"Yes, and then I have to go someplace else to see a man called Walter Brent."

No more responding to that than she had to the previous line, Mimi asked, "And *then?*"

She looked, Apple self-urged, like a working girl who wanted nothing other than to have a fling on the Riviera. He said, "Then I can come back here, at about five."

"Why don't we meet elsewhere at that time?" the girl said, brightening back to fresh from the staleness she had started to show. "For a drink or something."

Apple nodded slowly, as though agreeing that although history did repeat itself, it didn't necessarily do so by design or whim.

Mimi said, "We could come here afterwards."

"Where shall we meet?"

"At the Bunker."

"Wherever that might be."

While she was explaining that the huge auditorium built on the Croisette for the Film Festival had been so dubbed by the press because of its brute ugliness, Mimi stood up, on the bed, and stretched.

Apple leaned forward yearningly. There was a whimper in his eyes and an upbeat in his pulses. He said, "I might just take a siesta after all."

"Fine, Tom," Mimi said, springing lightly to the floor. "Then you'll be nice and fresh for later." Within half a minute she was gone, still nude, scooped-up clothes under one arm. Her last words were, "The Bunker at five."

Apple went to the telephone. "Cold shower," he muttered repeatedly until he was connected with the desk. Yes, the proprietress said, the dark young lady whom Monsieur had passed in the hall had checked in at noon.

That left the matter of the key, Apple mused after disconnecting, and was gratified to find himself accepting that other keys might fit this door or that the maid could have left the room unlocked.

So, Mimi's presence here being possibly an accident, Apple thought, the next step would be to see if she went through with the date.

Apple went into the bathroom for that shower which no longer needed to be cold. When he was undressed he heard the telephone ring. Absently he picked up Bernard, whom he put on as he went out to the instrument and tugged straight before lifting the receiver.

"Hello, One," the caller said.

Although Apple recognised the voice as belonging to the Brit agent who had accosted him in the Carlton Bar, he said, "You have the wrong number."

"Too bad. I can't pass on my bit of news to our man in Cannes."

"Okay okay. What's the news?"

"If you posted anything of consequence today," the agent said, "you're in trouble."

"You're going to tell me why, of course."

"Thieves, in quotes, smashed that corner mailbox with a truck and took all the mail."

Apple said, "What an excellent idea."

"So what did you send off today?"

"A picture postcard to my dog."

"You're a riot," the man said bitterly. The line died.

It was ten minutes to five. Neat in flannels and a blazer, his shirt open at the neck, Apple walked toward the Croisette. He felt refreshed, relaxed, ready for come what may. Bernard had been thoroughly combed.

Strolling, Apple spared a thought for his blunt attitude toward the Brit, both on the telephone and when they had met in the bar. Acknowledging that although he had pretended this was to try to play the cool pro, he told himself now it was actually to hide the fact that he felt sorry for the agent; he didn't like sentimentality, and pity was an offensive emotion when unrequested by the pitied.

By musing along these satisfying lines, agreeing at the same time how good and unique it was to be brutally honest with oneself, Apple was able to avoid the underlying truth: that his bluntness said in essence Keep Off. In a dark closet of his mind he knew that, as in any trade or profession, everyone wanted to climb, so if given half a chance, would push you out and take over your place. In the spy business your greatest enemy could be a colleague.

Humming, his romantic view of espionage kept intact by his not looking in that closet, Apple turned onto the Croisette. He headed west. When traffic eased he crossed to the pavement beside the sea.

Ahead, the promenade started to widen. It went on doing so until you could have played football around where stood the Bunker, a building of macho intent which Apple found not unpleasant. He stopped when a ball-kick away, the better to do a surveying.

When his eyes reached a fronting flight of steps, broad as a street, Apple saw Mimi. She stood on the middle step looking around with a hand making a can-

opy over her gaze like a lost Indian. She was as incon-
spicuous as an elephant on roller-skates in her bright
red jeans, tangerine shirt and scarf of emerald green.
Apple waved.

Not responding, Mimi continued to look for the tribe.
Next, still not having seen the waver, she lowered her
arm and started to amble down the steps.

Apple went forward. He had to take a devious path
between the people who stood or strolled on this popular place for constitutionals and gossip.

Over heads, Apple saw Mimi check with her wristwatch as she came to a slow halt. She was near the
roadway. It was when she looked up again that the grey
car came to a zoom-fast stop nearby.

Surprise brought Apple to a teetering standstill as
from the car leapt a man. He was tall and sturdy and
wore the whites of an able seaman. Running the few
metres to Mimi, he grabbed her by the arm.

She looked stunned. Poor resistance she offered,
merely tottering as she was dragged to the car, stum-
bling on being bundled inside. It happened at top
speed. The car shot off even before Sailor had pulled
the door closed.

"Hey!" Apple shouted, his surprise finally gone. He
charged forward into a run. Veering right to aim for the
car, which was coming this way, he bumped into a fat
man who wore a black dress that reached the ground.

Apple said, "Sorry."

The priest clasped him by both shoulders and asked a
startled, "What's wrong?"

Apple told him, "Nothing is." He swung him around
as though they were doing a dance, broke free and
turned toward the road, running again.

The grey car was ten metres away, level, in the process of going by, Mimi struggling in the back with Sailor. The driver was Bullybeef.

Apple kept going. He reached and went into the roadway, where the grey car was drawing ahead, passing other vehicles. Following at an insipid run, the act a gesture, automatic, Apple glanced behind.

By that same magic that works against need, making taxicabs disappear with the first drop of rain, the traffic of a minute ago had been reduced to a single motorcycle.

There was still traffic the other way, in front of the snatch car, preventing it from building up speed. All, Apple knew, was not lost, though no way was he going to be able to catch up on foot. He had to find wheels.

Again Apple looked behind. The motorcycle was closer. The two young long-haired blond people aboard in shorts and T-shirts Apple took for females, next for males, and then saw, as the bike drew abreast, that they were girl and boy.

He moved close. Running alongside, he panted about an emergency. The boy, in front, said, "I think this guy's crazy." The girl said, "No, he's drunk." The language they spoke was Finnish.

In the same language Apple said, "Not crazy, not drunk. I need help. My wife's in a grey car up there and I've got to catch up. She's with her lover."

While the girl called the lover a bastard and the boy called the wife a bitch, Apple suggested he be loaned the motorbike. That was ignored.

"Hop on," the girl said, reaching for him. At the same time the boy veered his machine closer and reached out also. Apple found himself being pulled onto the bike between the pair of them. He finished up prone, stomach on the girl's thighs, upper body sticking out one way and lower the other.

The motorcycle picked up speed at once. With growing alarm Apple watched the ground three feet distant go zipping by. He prayed he would maintain his precarious balance. There was nothing to hold on to. When he tried with his right hand, the boy pushed it away from the handlebar; on trying with his left, it was slapped off the girl's shorts. He reached down to a pipe and got burned.

To pass a car the bike swerved gracefully, leaning. Apple's face came within a foot of the flashing tarmac. Petrified, he shouted to forget the whole thing, he had been joking, he wasn't even married. His words went unheard in the batter of wind and the engine's roar.

Again the motorcycle keeled, this time the other way. The toecap of Apple's left shoe clapped against the ground. On the instant he raised his legs, which sent him sinking at the far end. He moaned.

The ride went on. With Apple continually see-sawing, moaning and asking for help from a deity in whom he didn't believe, the motorcycle swept along through traffic. Apple's view was restricted. When he did manage to turn enough to see ahead, the view was side-on and distorted and it did nothing to assist his spirits.

The bike steered between two vehicles. Apple's head was inches away from one and he felt his shoes snicker off the other. He wondered if he should forget the moan, try a scream.

Faintly, he could hear the girl singing. More obvious and a boost to the torment was her time-beating: the thump of a fist in the small of his back and the up-jerk of one thigh near his groin.

They left the Croisette. Zagging and keeling, they

went along a narrow street at speed. The girl thumped, jerked, sang. Apple closed his eyes.

When he opened them again it was because the bike had commenced a fast heart-squeezing halt. It was still moving as he felt himself being pulled upright, had stopped by the time his feet touched the ground. He staggered free. His legs were trembling.

Turning in the direction pointed out by the boy, Apple saw a grey car stopping in a side street. It was a different shade, a different make, a different size, a different nationality, and the occupants, a middle-aged couple, were different people.

Apple turned back. The young blondes were smiling, proud of success, glad of having been able to help. In unison they asked, "All right?" Nodding, Apple thanked them sincerely.

FOUR

Apple had nothing against Spanish cuisine. Certainly he had enjoyed the meal of gazpacho and paella which he was now rounding off with a coffee. It was just that he had expected something else of the restaurant when he had seen on its frontage a model of the Eiffel Tower.

The metre-high structure, however, according to the Spanish waiter, had been bought and set out there only today to show how nationalistic they were, Frenchly so. Terrorists had been at work locally, for a change directing their efforts at the tourism-orientated: a taxi window had been blasted, a mailbox had been wrecked, tourists were being abducted in cars and on motorcycles.

"I don't believe it myself," the waiter had confided. "But that's what people're saying, and the boss, he's ready to believe anything."

Apple sipped his coffee. He was relaxed, recovered from his bike misadventure and sure of being free of immediate danger, no problem over whether to leave from front or back. He knew he hadn't been followed here.

When, after leaving the Finns, he had done a Lizard (tail shedding) before slipping into a cinema, Apple had taken Bernard off. He had stayed uncovered for his two hours of moviegoing and, with blazer removed to further change image, during his walk to the nearest likely-looking restaurant. Here, he had put blazer and Bernard back on while entering.

Apple now went over his mullings. Three nondates in a row was too much of a coincidence, even without the circumstantial evidence of the first two—a commotion outside the railway station, a car slowing beside Tilda as she waited. So it was safe to assume that all three girls had been snatched.

Apple snapped his fingers, got up smartly, went at a stride to the corner telephone box. This act of efficiency was to cover the embarrassing fact that he was doing what should have been done hours ago.

The proprietress answered. No, the dark young lady from Paris was no longer registered—alas, if Monsieur had been hit by Cupid's arrow. A messenger had come to collect her things and pay the bill.

Back at his table Apple allowed himself to feel relieved. The delay made no difference. Mimi had no doubt gone the same route as Susan and Tilda.

Although Apple knew it was entirely possible for this route to have no connexion with himself or the Property, that some other manner of villainy was afoot, he felt it must be the work either of the Competition or Owner. Whomever, the motive for abducting would be to question the girls about the man they were waiting for. What was he up to? Was he really Walter Brent? When the girls proved to be blank on information, they would be released and told to fade.

As to how the whomever had got on to them in the first place, that, Apple had concluded, was by range-finder microphone. He and each girl had been heard making a date, and the Bullybeef team had got there first.

Apple was in possession of a plot. He had been planning neatly and felt he was backing a winner, which meant giving the team another chance with another girl.

Apple would allow himself to be seen, tailed. He would pick a likely girl of the newspaper persuasion, offer her an interview and make a date, cancel it later, privately, and go alone to the rendezvous.

What, exactly, Apple intended doing then he hadn't given any consideration to. He just liked the neat planning.

Bill paid, waiter congratulated on his sensibleness in not believing absurd rumours, Apple left. At a bold walk he went along the street, where lights were on against the first suggestions of dusk.

Over the following hour, wandering streets broad and narrow, Apple made progress, he told himself. He felt he had collected at least one hound; he got smartly out of talking to two Brent-seeking Greek pressmen by telling them, in their own language, that he was a simple businessman from Athens; he saw and considered several prospects for his plan while denying that the reason he didn't approach them was because of his personal noncaper preference for something more attractive.

He found her.

She was sitting at a sidewalk café, alone yet without the stamp of loneliness, that pugnacious clench which dares observers to regard the solo as lonely. Her decor was blue. Boots, stockings, short skirt, shirt and bolero top—blue. Her brown hair accepted that it was undistinguished, but her face had an unusual elegance.

Nearing at his leisure, Apple was willing to admit to being drawn partly by the setting's theatricality. Fully dark now, lights were on strongly under the café canopy, lending it the appearance of a stage.

That the girl was press showed by the plasticated card fixed to her chest and the lordly way she was reading a newspaper. That she was probably Anglo-Saxon of the non-American strain showed in the primness of her mouth.

When Apple stopped beside the table he read on her card that she was Linda Dexter of the Tigi-Tagi *Weekly Yarn*. He asked, "New South Wales?"

The girl looked up lazily. "That's right, sport," she said after giving him a thorough once-over. "You know it like the back of your hand and you want to sit down and chat about good old days there."

"I've never been anywhere in Australia in my life."

"Okay then. You're the head of an important news agency and you want to hire me for the Paris office at a megabucks salary."

"Me, I'm not the head of anything."

"Then you must be somebody famous that every reporter'd sell his left nostril to interview and you're going to give me that big fat scoop."

"Well," Apple said, "yes." He was intrigued by the wisecrack glibness, challenged by the attack of the cliché *sport*.

"I knew it," the girl said in bored triumph. "I've heard 'em all."

"Let me introduce myself. I'm Walter Brent, Ms. Dexter. Does that mean anything to you?"

"No. Is all that hair for real?"

"It used to be when it was on other people, growing. I'm incognito. I generally am when away from home."

"Go on, sport, lay it on thick. If it wasn't for the hair to hide the old phizog, you'd be getting mobbed. I didn't ask you to sit down."

Apple didn't realise he had. He began to get up with an automatic, "Sorry."

"Stay, stay, it's better than breaking my neck looking up," the girl said. "Maybe you're famous for being tall, Wally-o. Call me Linda."

"I'm not famous in the widespread sense and I wouldn't be mobbed if people saw my face. But I am well-known in a special field, that of the convention here."

She nodded. "A bookworm. As a matter of fact, I saw you at the Lincoln reception."

"I wear a disguise, Linda, because reporters and others can be a nuisance."

"Sounds good. You might even be genuine."

"So might you. How come you're covering a convention of, to use your term, bookworms, if you know so little about the field you've never heard of Walter Brent?"

"The dealer?"

"The eccentric collector."

The girl said, "I'm doing Europe in six months, covering all the major convention centres but off-season. Frankfurt when it's not the book fair, Cannes without movies."

"Sounds good."

"Thanks, Wally-o."

They contemplated one another steadily. Apple, attracted, asked, "Are men always trying to pick you up?" As all along, conscious that a microphone could be eavesdropping, he spoke with clear enunciation. "You act as if it were so."

"No, but when a guy comes up out of the night like this, what he's up to can't be any good."

"What I'm up to is boringly respectable, Linda. I do have to give an interview while I'm here, it's standard, so it might as well be to someone who's nice to look at."

"Flattery, Wally-o, will get you off the starting-blocks."

"What I suggest is, you call your editor and ask him if he'd like a piece on Walter Brent. Then we could set a time to meet, say tomorrow morning."

Linda looked at him carefully. "You don't want to wine me and dine me at once?"

"I've had dinner," Apple said. "Anyway, I'm sure you're not the kind of girl who'd go out with a perfect stranger, are you?"

"Sport, I'd go out with an imperfect friend if I fancied him. But that's beside the point. Y'know, maybe I ought to make that call."

Some minutes later, walking along the street toward his companion's hotel, Apple said, "The outcome of your telephone call being a foregone conclusion, where shall we meet?"

"The hotel lobby, at eleven-thirty."

"The time's fine, the place is out. There're other press people staying there, I'm sure."

"If you're trying to propose your room or mine . . ."

"No-man's land," Apple said. Speaking clearly, he went on to suggest a certain corner on Rue d'Antibes.

Linda looked up at him, asking, "You want us to meet outside, on the street?"

"Sure."

"Yes, you're pretty eccentric, all right."

At nine o'clock the following morning, using his Thomas Wainwright credit card, Apple rented a car. The crux of his plan, he had decided, was to follow the snatchers when, empty of hand, they left the rendezvous.

Last night, on his return to the Mérimée, Apple had tried to contact Linda by telephone at her hotel in order to change, not cancel, their date. She wasn't in. He would see to that matter later this morning.

The idea of being early abroad was to find a convenient parking slot. This Apple accomplished with so much ease that he was unable to feel clever. The rented Opel he parked around the next corner along from the one on which, the enemy thought, Linda would be waiting.

Car locked, Apple strolled down Rue d'Antibes. He told himself he had chosen well. Sided by expensive stores with smirky faces, kerbs guarded by huge plant pots to prevent parking, the slim and gracious street was a one-way thoroughfare with a steady flow of traffic. A car, speed dictated, could only come and leave in one direction.

It was nine-thirty when Apple stopped at the desk in Linda's hotel. His spirits took a pause in their chirp as he heard from the clerk that Miss Dexter had already gone out.

So what if she doesn't come back here but goes on to the rendezvous corner? Apple questioned as he sat on a couch to wait. What if she gets abducted? What if she gets hurt, abused, assaulted?

Stopping himself before he went too far, Apple got up and returned to the desk. The clerk could offer no information on Miss Dexter's movements.

Apple went outside, where, he reckoned, he could

still wait as well as have the chance of seeing Linda if she wandered by. Across the street was a café with large windows. Apple went in, asked the waiter for a Perrier, sat by a window where he had all angles covered.

He watched, fretted, fumed, chastised himself for having involved an innocent person in what could turn out to be something messy.

At ten o'clock Apple got another bottle of water, at ten-thirty a glass of lemonade, at a quarter to eleven a pain in his bladder. It had been coming on him for some time, though he had been trying to ignore it. He kept trying.

To make pain elsewhere, divertingly, he twisted his fingers and pulled hard on an earlobe. He dredged up oddments of titillating information such as the fact that budgerigars molt in October. He hummed a land chanty.

Nothing worked. The pain went on, growing stronger, yelling to be let out. But Apple knew that if he gave in, slipped back to the washroom, that was when Linda was bound to appear and he would miss her.

He hummed loudly, tapped his feet and squirmed. He swayed. He jiggled. He pretended being amused to recall that the world's first palindrome had been created in the Garden of Eden: Madam, I'm Adam. His head baked steadily inside Bernard.

A waiter came to ask solicitously if everything were all right, Apple jiggled and swayed while answering with eleven fast different forms of the affirmative and a pair of middle-aged women strolling past the window slyly pointed him out to one another.

The crisis was brought to a crescendo by a small girl at the next table. She had been watching Apple during her pull at a milk shake through a straw. Now, nearing the bottom of the glass, she started to make slurp noises.

With a faint, continuing, groany laugh, Apple shot to his feet and swiftly trembled to the rear.

On returning front again, paler than usual, eyes dreamy, Apple found he had only five minutes left to zero-hour. Linda could be there already, even though she had said she was normally a little late, by design, as she thought being prompt showed lack of moral fibre.

Unaware of giving the small girl's mother a look of compassion as he passed, Apple left the café. He strode through the busy noon-nearing streets and soon came onto Rue d'Antibes, where he turned toward the rendezvous spot.

It came into view. Part of that view was Linda. She stood leaning nonchalantly on the wall, clear of the pedestrian stream. She was dressed the same as last night except her skirt had been changed for a pair of tight blue pants.

Apple slowed. The time being exactly eleven-thirty, he mused, the snatchers were sure to show up just as he got there, so, seeing him, they would go straight on by and the whole plan would come to nothing, since he couldn't very well drop Linda flat to go dashing off to get his car and give chase.

Therefore, Apple concluded, a better idea might be to wait until the snatchers were actually trying to pull off their abduction, then rush in and break it up.

What this would accomplish in respect of the caper Apple didn't venture to consider. He liked the plan's boldness. Also he liked having the opportunity to play hero, but he wasn't giving that the faintest recognition and would have denied in heat any suggestion of its existence.

Half a block from the rendezvous corner, on the street's opposite side, Apple stepped into a shop doorway. In front of him was a constant, sluggish stream of single-lane traffic. He divided his attention between it and Linda after he had sunk to one knee in the act of attending to a shoelace to be less visible.

That paid off. Bullybeef didn't glance aside when he drove past, casually steering a black Jaguar, his elbow on the sill. Whoever was the one person in the back Apple failed to establish because of dark-tinted windows. In readiness he got up and stepped out of his doorway.

The Jaguar halted by the corner. Its back door opened. No one emerged. Linda, however, glanced that way as if called. She went across. She looked down into the car. She smiled. She nodded. She spoke. She stooped. She got in.

The car moved on.

After blinking slowly and dully for a moment, his mouth ajar, Apple snapped into action. He ran the half block to the corner around which he had left the Opel, raced to the car, dithered it unlocked and fought his ranginess inside.

When, driving forward, Apple reached the corner, he spurted cheekily in front of a taxi. Braking with a squeal, the cabbie yelled terrible things about the mothers of tourists. Apple ignored him. One-handed he fiddled with the sliding roof to get it open so he could stand up, look ahead and pinpoint the sleek black car, which he had no intentions of losing.

The scene would have been more appealing if it had lacked sinister connotations. Even so, Apple, arriving in his crouch behind a stack of lobster pots, couldn't help but admire the launch as it sped bouncily toward a large white motor yacht preening itself some five hundred metres out.

He wasn't absolutely certain that the launch held those who had been in the Jaguar, parked untidily near him on the concrete slipway, but he reckoned his assumption was too right to be wrong.

The launch, seeming to shrink in size, slowed as it drew close to the yacht and then went out of sight around her far side, where, Apple guessed, there would be a gangway. Somehow or another he would get to use it himself.

Rising, Apple looked around at this nontouristic area of shoreline. Apart from a man with a fishing rod in the distance, there was nobody about. Nearby, lying on the slipway, was a rowboat. It looked reliable.

To decide between borrowing the boat or asking the angler if he knew anything about its owner, Apple tossed a mental coin, one he had used before. It had two heads. Due to being confused by excitement he chose tails as the winner. Giving up on the whole foolishness he went to the boat and began to drag it down the concrete.

Another minute and Apple was out on the water, rowing steadily but prepared to pick up the beat if someone should appear and shout a stop-thief.

Frequent glances behind showed him no observers on the yacht, whose swordfish bow he passed under silently. The launch bobbed beside a stairway.

Shipping his oars for quietness and letting impetus take him on, Apple paddled with his hands to make a final berthing by the gangway's underside. Rowboat tied, he swung around onto the steps. He went up at a creep.

This he maintained on deck to go along beside gleaming white superstructure. He heard nothing. A goodly section of his mind was occupied with standing off and seeing him adventurously employed thus.

A drone of voice brought Apple to a halt. Once he had gauged source he moved on, stopping again by the open porthole that was set at knee-level. After squatting, he peered cautiously in. He was looking down into a large saloon.

The voice belonged to Falcon. The ugly man, still in his fur-collared coat, was sitting on the right. From what could be seen of it from the downward and side-on angle, his face bore a pleased expression.

He said, "I promise you, my dear girl, you can believe these young ladies."

Sitting centrally, facingly, on a long white couch, were Susan, Tilda and Mimi. They, too, looked complacent. American Tilda was chewing a toothpick. Canadian Susan fiddled with a hank of her long blond hair. French Mimi was smoking.

Not complacent in the least was Linda. She sat on the left, opposite Falcon; sat on the edge of her chair, hands gripping its carved arms. One of her ankles was shackled to a carved leg.

Glaring at the ugly man, Linda grated, "You may have got this lot in your power, with drugs or whatever, but you're going to have problems with me."

"My dear girl," Falcon said, "you really must try to curb your love of the melodramatic." He spoke English with a badly bruised accent.

"This isn't exactly an everyday occurrence, sport."

"That I will grant you."

One of the girls on the couch yawned, one scratched an elbow and the third took a casual glance at her wristwatch. Linda said, "Or maybe they're part of the team, like those two in the car."

"I believe I have already stated," Falcon said, "that we are one happy family."

"In the vice game."

"Vice, my dear?"

"Listen," Linda said toughly. "I'm no nit-brain, you know. If this isn't what they used to call white slavery, I'm a piece of string."

"Then I shall keep you free of knots," Falcon said with a chuckle. He aimed his ugliness toward the trio on the couch. "Who was it who said I had no sense of humour?"

Immediately attentive, the three shook their heads and smiled in ridicule. The act had a strong suggestion of subordination, it seemed to Apple, who, with part of his mind, was still trying to place Falcon's accent.

"You're as funny as a flat tyre," Linda said.

Falcon: "The only thing that amuses Australians, I have heard, is a dying rabbit in the pouch of a dead kangaroo."

"Two flat tyres."

"But enough of this frivolity, my dear. I sincerely wish to put your fears at rest. This situation has nothing to do with white slavery, with vice of any kind, and you will come to no harm whatever."

"I bet."

"I mean it seriously. You will be my guest on this comfortable little yacht for a short time, and then re-leased none the worse for your experience."

Linda rattled her ankle fastening, folded her arms. "I don't get it."

"You will when I have explained."

"So get on with it, sport."

As Falcon leaned back and placed his bony fingertips together, Apple was visited by a jab of recognition. Although he didn't understand the cause, he was intrigued still further.

Falcon said, "The young lady there with the nice tan, using the name of Susan, playing a Canadian reporter, approached Mr. Walter Brent and succeeded in making a date with him. It was outdoors, in a public place. Perhaps, Susan, you could tell Miss Dexter why you did that."

The girl said, "It was so I could be abducted, dragged off struggling in a car."

Linda shook her head. "Sure. Real clear."

"For the same reason," Falcon said, "the other two clever girls also established themselves with Mr. Walter Brent and were able to get him to agree to meetings, again in outdoor public places. But alas."

Linda said, "Never mind alas, sport. Why all these phony abductions?"

"Obviously for Mr. Walter Brent's benefit. To have him give chase, play the gallant."

"And walk into a trap?"

Briefly, Falcon separated his hands in order to make a gesture of offering, of thanks. "You are perceptive, my dear. For which I am grateful."

"Then just unlock this cuff," Linda said. "And I'll be on my merry way."

It was when Falcon ignored her, going on to talk of Mr. Walter Brent himself being too large and strong for an abduction, that Apple drew clues together. The man reminded him of Angus Watkin and the accent was Russian. Falcon had to be KGB, a senior Hammer, a Control, in fact. Which made the three women Sickles.

"Although, a rival of mine did try it, a direct kidnapping," the ugly man said. "He used a stolen taxi. Unfortunately, the project failed."

Linda said, "You know, all this begins to sound to me like industrial espionage."

Again Falcon did that flowering with his hands. "Something along those lines," he said. "But let us not get sidetracked on to them. I believe I was on the subject of alas."

"Alas away."

"Awkwardly for abduction, Mr. Walter Brent happened to look the other way when Susan was taken, at the railway station. When it was Tilda's turn, on the Croisette, he walked off into a side street at the crucial moment. With Mimi he did manage to not miss seeing the abduction, but, aided by youngsters on a motorcycle, he followed the wrong car."

Linda said, "He's not stupid, is he?"

Ignoringly: "Next in our travail we had a waiter listen to yourself and Mr. Walter Brent last night as you sat together at a sidewalk café and as you walked to a hotel. A date was made to meet on Rue d'Antibes—and, of course, you more or less know the rest."

"Was the car followed?"

"Yes. Mr. Walter Brent was prepared, as it turned out. No doubt he intended taking you for a drive. He had a rented vehicle. And, although he almost took two wrong turnings, he did find his way to the docks. There, we had arranged for a rowing boat to be conveniently at hand."

Linda looked around quickly. "He's here?"

Falcon nodded. "He is, my dear."

"Where?"

"He is watching and listening at one of those portholes up there. Which is the reason I have gone to the trouble of explaining matters. Now I won't have to go through it again with Mr. Walter Brent."

Still looking from one porthole to another, Linda yelled, "Run, Wally-o!"

"That will serve no purpose," the ugly man said, calm. "Reginald and Percy are on hand and will see to it that Mr. Walter Brent accepts the invitation to be my guest."

That his presence was known about had been slowly dawning on Apple, so he was unsurprised to hear this stated. He was still without surprise on turning from the porthole, looking ahead and seeing Bullybeef, who was leaning on the handrail, smiling like a fed glutton.

Not moving out of his crouch, Apple looked the other way. Now he did get a shock. Standing there was himself.

Several strange seconds passed before Apple understood, saw everything as normal. He wasn't insane or hallucinating. The man, similar height to himself, with similar features, wearing similar clothes, had on a hairpiece similar to Bernard. He was impersonating Apple impersonating Thomas Wainwright impersonating Walter Brent.

During those same seconds questions were answered for Apple. Why Falcon had gazed at him that time so searchingly from the moving Rolls-Royce (to note details in preparing Double). Why Linda had willingly got into the Jaguar (she thought the hairy man sitting in its rear was the person she had a date with). Why this ambush was necessary (to remove the assumed Walter Brent from circulation so that Double could take his place, as there would be no point in having two Brents around, both trying to contact Owner).

It was all good spy stuff, Apple had to admit, but

admiration would come later. What he had to do now was choose between going in for a bit of fancy combat or a quick dive overboard.

Apple began to rise. Midway up he stopped with a gasp of pain. One of his legs had gone to sleep.

The stateroom, of ample proportions, had white furniture, a bed coverlet of the same colour and carpeting that would have matched if it hadn't been for wear and tear. Apple felt vaguely angelic as well as a shade criminal, the latter due to his manacle, even though the form of attachment was unorthodox. One cuff was around his left wrist and the other was around his right ankle.

Apple acknowledged that the beauty of this standard KGB method of restraint, called Quasimodo, was that, so long as he didn't stand up, the prisoner was inconvenienced but little in his manual doings, which meant less work for the jailer; yet ambulatory movement was limited, much more so than if the feet were shackled together, in which case the prisoner could at least bound; this way, the best he could do was crouch along in awkward swings.

A further point in favour of Quasimodo, Apple mused, was that the handcuffs couldn't be used as a weapon, for striking or strangling, in those ways he had been taught at Damian House. So he could stop thinking escape from that angle and concentrate on something else.

But there was no something else on which to concentrate. In the half hour since being carried here by Bullybeef and Double, his leg screeching, Apple had checked the stateroom out thoroughly. It seemed impregnable.

One porthole, open, was the size of a tennis ball. The

other, welded shut, had glass thick enough to resist all but the heaviest of blunt instruments. There was nothing of that nature available either here or in the tiny lavatory, and as for furniture, what wasn't built in was bolted down. The door, flush with the wall, had no handle on this side.

Apple, sitting on the bed edge, left arm plunged low, sighed. But he wasn't seriously despondent. For one thing, his masquerade had succeeded. For another, neither he nor Linda was in danger, since they posed no threat to the KGB team—so long as they were safely out of the way, here, and it wasn't suspected that the male of the two was a Brit. For a third thing, he didn't think Double could pull the impersonation off, if, as Apple believed, contact had already been made with Owner.

There were sounds beyond the door. Next, it opened. In came Bullbeef, who still wore the same seaman's sweater. His wrestler features in a two-out-of-three smirk, he took up a stance on the threshold.

Around him into view came Falcon. He stayed there. Bowing toward Apple he said, "Good evening, Mr. Walter Brent. We meet at last."

Acting anger under control, Apple said, "I'll give you five minutes to let me out of here."

"That, obviously, I am not about to do. But with luck you shouldn't be my guest for too long. I imagine a couple of days at the outside."

"The police're going to hear about this."

"Naturally. But by that time we will be gone. In any case, the police know what strange creatures we collectors are, forever conniving against one another. They will be amused rather than goaded into action."

"I had an idea it wasn't industrial espionage," Apple said. "And I begin to see the light."

"Of course you do."

"That tall man in the wig and beard. He's going to take my place, in case the seller shows up."

"The seller?"

Playing irritated, Apple said, "Come on, don't pretend you don't know what I'm talking about. All this can only be in connexion with one thing—the Sherlock Holmes manuscript."

Falcon bowed again. "Precisely, Mr. Walter Brent. I am just as avid as yourself to get hold of Sir Arthur Conan Doyle's exposé for my collection."

Allowing what he hoped was a crafty expression to come into his eyes, Apple said, "Maybe we can make a deal. Maybe we could work together."

"No deals, no partnerships. Sorry. I will succeed alone. For a quiet-living person, I am not unresourceful."

"I'll bet you're not," Apple grumbled like someone whose ploy had failed. "I'll bet Madam X is one of your tricks, like Tilda and Susan and Mimi."

"Tricks, sir?"

"Sure. That note could've been sent me by you, a red-herring to get me out of the way."

Falcon smiled quietly. Apple knew that smile. He had seen it on Angus Watkin when he, too, like all Controls, wanted to have it believed that he was aware of everything.

Apple nodded. "I thought so. And while I was on a wild-goose chase in Nice to meet the mysterious Madam X outside the post office at three o'clock today, my impersonator would be having the convention to himself."

As though to apologise for being clever, Falcon did the offering with his hands. "One tries."

Apple said, "But then I made the date with Linda and you were able to pull off your ambush trick finally." He tutted. "I had high hopes of the Nice deal."

"I'm delighted that I made the note convincing."

Sourly: "Oh, you did, you did."

Falcon asked, "And tell me, did I give the lady a realistic description?"

"Oh yes. Fittingly glamorous. Black pantsuit and—" Apple, not wanting to make it too neat, broke off. He snapped his fingers. "Damn."

"I beg your pardon?"

"Too bad I destroyed that note. I would've had a sample of your handwriting. Also, it would be a highly collectible piece of writing in connexion with this affair."

"Quite so," Falcon said. "But do please continue with the way I described the mystery lady. I love critiques of my literary efforts."

Sneering: "Really?"

"Don't all collectors? As I am sure you are aware, we are all frustrated writers. That's the source of our passion—or mania, if you wish. Ownership is a form of authorship."

"You're entitled to your opinion."

Falcon said, "But to Madam X. The way I described her."

Apple shrugged. "It doesn't matter." Falcon, he knew, couldn't press for details without giving away his ignorance, and in any case had enough to go on with the clothes, the time, the place.

Apple knew further that his gambit had worked, if only because the Control couldn't afford to risk treating it as simply that, a gambit, which he certainly would have done had he known he was dealing with an operative. Therefore some of the team would be drawn away to cover the Nice possibility, weakening the guard here.

"It matters not at all, true," Falcon said. "Anyway, I mustn't take up any more of your time."

"Thoughtful of you."

"The reason I stopped in was to assure you that you are quite safe. I wish you no harm."

"Gee thanks."

"Please make yourself completely at home. Do take off that hairy ensemble, if you are so inclined. It cannot be all that comfortable."

"It isn't, to tell the truth."

Without turning, Falcon pointed over his shoulder. "The bell there, it will summon service, should there be anything you require to make your stay more pleasant."

"I'll try to be inventive."

"You and Miss Dexter will be meeting for lunch. I have instructed my chef to prepare something special."

"Well now."

"What he doesn't know about Cantonese cuisine is not worth knowing." He turned away. "Until later."

Apple, his chin at thigh level, swung along the corridor like an ape keeping his ankle-bell from ringing. His gait was being matched in rhythm with a tune whistled derisively by Bullybeef, who came along behind. Apple didn't care. He was glad of the change of scene.

Over the past hour all that had happened was an experiment with room-service. After a touch of the bell a voice out of nowhere had said, "Your desire, sir?" and, to Apple's request for a bottle of mineral water, "Yes, sir." Minutes later a hidden wall-panel had slid aside to reveal a recess, within it a bottle and a cup, both plastic. These removed, the panel had closed again and had resisted, rocklike, Apple's attempts to get it open. His next request, to have Tilda, Mimi and Susan come in to dance for him, wearing only nail-polish, had received no answer.

The dining saloon continued the elsewhere luxury and colour scheme. Instead of the twelve settings it could easily manage, the long white table had two, one at either end. Linda was already there. In addition to a Quasimodo, which made her appear to be extra careful about arm-off-the-table manners, she was shackled at her free ankle to the chair leg.

While the same precaution was being applied by Bullybeef to Apple, once he was in position at the table's other end, Linda asked. "Are you who I think you are?" His entrance she had watched coolly.

Nodding, Apple touched his naked face. "It's a nice change. I've been inside that thing for days."

"I recognise your voice," Linda said. "Otherwise I wouldn't believe it was you." There was no change in her cool attitude.

"Lucky for me you've got a good ear."

"But not that I've got a good eye. Frankly, I think you look better with most of your face hidden."

"Oh," Apple said. He would have straightened in offence and defence except for the Quasimodo hold. When Bullybeef had left the saloon, he asked, "Is something wrong?"

Looking around: "It gets me into this bloody mess and then it asks if there's something wrong. Christ."

With an uncomfortable roll of his shoulders, Apple

said, "Yes, I see what you mean, Linda. Thick of me. I'd forgotten I owe you an apology."

Glaring: "I'll say you do."

"Well . . ."

"It's not as though what happened was accidental, something that couldn't be helped. You *planned* it."

"Well . . ."

"You picked me up at that sidewalk café for one reason only, Mr. Walter bloody Brent. That reason was to be your patsy. You *used* me."

"Well . . ."

"Go on, deny it."

Apple gazed at her, feeling helpless and fighting off a threat of blush. He wished he could come up with a brilliant lie, which, if his mind wasn't stupidly occupied with that wish, he was perfectly capable of doing—with someone he disliked, which told him he must like Linda more than he realised. When, the seconds ticking by, he couldn't think of a lie that was even shiny, let alone brilliant, he knew he had the beginnings of a bad case.

Linda said, "You're gaping like a fish."

Fumbling with words like a poet reading a friend's verse, Apple started on explanation and apology. He continued despite the impassive uniformed steward who came in with the first course, claiming subconscious motivation.

He ended, "I guess I must've realised something funny was going on with there elusive no-show girls without seeing it on the surface."

"So you approached me, you chatted me up and you made a date to meet me at a suitable spot for abduction, all without seeing what you were up to. Oh yes. Try another one, sport."

"That's all it could have been, Linda. I could spin you a good-sounding story, if you like, but—"

"Wouldn't have to be too good to beat that one."

"—I prefer the truth, and the only reason I had for approaching you at the café was because you took my fancy."

Linda waved her free hand, which held a spoon. "Forget it for now," she said. "If I weren't so hungry, I'd throw this soup at you."

They began the meal. While joining in an erratic duologue about bird's-nesting, Apple, settling, got around to recognising that the crockery and drinking vessels were made of soft plastic and the cutlery was only spoons.

There wasn't much that could be used as a weapon, Apple allowed, if a guest should grab the steward and hold him as a hostage against release. Even though such a move would hardly be expected from the innocuous Walter Brent, Falcon was taking no chances. The Conan Doyle manuscript had mammoth value in the propaganda war.

After the second course of shredded pork with bean sprouts on pineapple rings had been served, and eclipsed, Linda said, "That's better. Food hath charms to soothe, et cetera, et cetera."

Apple asked, "You don't hate me anymore?"

"I hate nothing at this plump moment."

"Then maybe you're going to forgive me."

"Depends," Linda said. "I don't want to hear any more lies."

"Ask me anything you like."

"Okay then. Was I right in pegging this business for industrial espionage?"

"In a sense, yes," Apple said. "The industry in question being, of course, that which is connected with the convention. The written word."

"Sure. Some first editions can be worth big money."

"Right. It can be a pretty cutthroat business. But prestige is just as important as the financial angle."

Again Linda looked around the saloon, this time seeingly. "I should have asked you earlier, but do you think this place is bugged?"

Apple almost answered with what he believed to be the truth, an affirmative. He saw the bugging of cabins as not only inevitable but obvious. Firstly, that room-service voice showed the presence of speakers, which presumed the reverse, microphones. Secondly, the dining guests were placed far enough apart so that they had to speak clearly. Thirdly, everything showed that Falcon was too thorough to forego the chance to eavesdrop.

"No," Apple said, smiling in case there were also hidden cameras. "Our host isn't an evil mastermind, just a very determined collector. We may talk freely."

Which they did, about how pleasant the weather was in Cannes, until they were alone again after the steward had gone, leaving each with a marbled egg on a mound of rice.

"Okay," Linda said. "Let's have it. What does our host want that you've got?"

"I don't have it yet. Let's say it's a first edition, which in a way it is. I don't want to go into details, it's too much like counting chickens. And all this is off the record anyway."

"Check. Off the record. First-edition-type thing. So you two are after the same one."

"We are. And while I'm a prisoner here he'll be trying to locate the seller by having someone impersonate me.

That guy in the Jaguar wasn't doing a Walter Brent simply to get you in the car, y'know."

Linda nodded slowly. "Beautiful."

"He'll be doing his act all over town. But he doesn't know who the seller is."

"And you do?"

"Almost," Apple said. "It has to be one of two people." He hoped all this was being taped. "Either a woman I was supposed to meet in Nice this afternoon, or a man here in Cannes."

"A woman, eh?"

"A mystery. I know nothing about her."

Linda said, "But the man you know."

"Better than the woman, at least."

"Who is he?"

Apple chewed a mouthful of food while deciding who to use as the next red herring. That he chose Wiley was because of him being so obviously not Owner, as well as the fact that he would probably enjoy being cultivated by Falcon.

Swallowing, Apple said, "I don't know his name, but he's an Oriental." He went on to give a description. "Looks a bit like Charlie Chan—if you know your late, late movies."

"I do. Maybe you mean Mr. Moto or Mr. Wong. They sound more like the man you describe."

"Chan," Apple said, chin firm like a held chew. "Created by Earl Derr Biggers and based on a real-life Chinese detective called Chang Apana."

"You sound as though you might know what you're talking about, Wally-o."

"I do. The series started in 1931."

"Rubbish," Linda said cheerfully. "It was a serial before it was a series, it started in 1926 and the actor who played the minor role of Charlie Chan was called George Kuwa." She pushed her empty plate away and smiled. "You're doing your fish act again, sport."

All was silent, apart from the natural. Fittings creaked a complaint at having their stability tested. As if the sea adored its elegant visitor, waves came against the hull like lovers' tender slaps. Sea-gulls continually asked for more with their cry of me, me, me.

Apple was dangerously close to explaining to his smart side that although the Wiley lead would no doubt draw more of the guard away, it wasn't going to do him much good if he didn't soon get an idea on tackling the remainder, escaping.

By manacle necessity formed in a ball, Apple lay on his stateroom bed in a post-lunch haze. He didn't want to look at his watch because he knew three o'clock must be depressingly close. However, he did so now as a diversion from that nearing danger of seeing his smart side as shabby.

And failed to note the time on account of realising that he did, after all, have the article he had bemoaned his lack of: a pin. His haze clearing, he quickly moved to a sit on the edge of the bed.

It was the work of a minute to free one of the pins that held the strap to his wristwatch, which he then pocketed. The tiny implement, less than an inch long, would suffice as a lock picker, Apple knew from past but limited experience. He started on the ankle cuff, thus giving him the use of both hands.

Twenty minutes later, the tips of thumb and forefinger numb, eyes tired, bottom lip sore from being chewed, Apple hit the correct angle and the cuff came apart. After a rest he took care of the wrist end.

He was still looking at the defeated manacle in pride and satisfaction when a discreet noise sounded on the other side of the door.

Swiftly he put the cuffs back into place but without snicking their locks home. He sighed, sagged in an assumed expression of despondency.

The door opened a crack. At a curiously slow pace it eased inward until it was a foot from the jamb, at which stage a head began to appear. When it was fully in view Apple said an unenthusiastic, "You."

The Brit agent came farther in. "Nothing to it, One."

Apple tried, "What took you so long?"

"You were expecting me. Sure you were."

"I would've been here hours ago."

After the agent had played eye-crinkles, he waved the spray-can in his hand. "I think I got most of 'em."

Too late to stop himself, give away his ignorance, Apple asked, "What's that silly thing?"

"Knock-out mist. You give 'em one squirt and they drop. Your friends here'll be out for ten minutes."

Apple wasn't sure how to do nostalgia, but he tried to put some in his smile with, "Those old things're still being used? That's nice. I like to see traditions kept up."

The agent hummed lightly while putting the can in his pocket. He said, as though in sympathy, "You've still got your bracelets on. But then, it's only been two or three hours."

"Drugs," Apple said shortly. "I was doped."

"Oh yes?"

"I came to about five minutes ago."

Following another brief crinkling of the eyes, signalling amusement with kindness, the agent patted himself. "I believe I've got my skeleton with me."

"Why?"

"What?"

"We don't bother with those fiddly little things nowadays," Apple said, airy as a mentor. "Not if we've been through the modern section of Locks Five."

"Oh?"

"It's a tough course, pretty advanced, connected with sonics and resonances, but well worth the effort." Bending to the ankle cuff, he performed on it a series of taps, raps and finger-snaps, nail-flicks and knuckle-knocks. The cuff opened. The agent breathed in through his nose.

Whistling idly, Apple performed the same routine to part the other end. Manacle tossed aside, he got up and stretched. He managed not to allow himself to look at the Brit.

Who said, coldly, "When you've finished hanging around, One, we'll go."

"Sure, sure."

"We have about six minutes left before they start coming out of it."

Apple asked, "You have a boat?"

"If I'd swum here," the agent said, "I'd probably be wet."

"I suppose it's the only boat out there now."

"Yours was towed away by the launch."

Falcon was a real pro, Apple again acknowledged. He said, "Go wait in your boat. I have to get the girl."

"There's a doll I put to sleep up on deck."

"Another one. She's in a cabin down here."

"Sickle?"

"No," Apple said. "Off you go."

"Well, if you think you can manage . . ."

"One more thing. Got a gun?" Apple asked this knowing that, on this type caper, the agent would prob-

ably not be armed. He asked to pile on the pro-meets-
tyro business.

"Of course I have," the Brit said. "Haven't you?"

With a Watkin drawl, Apple told him, "For some reason I have never been able to fathom, prisoners are
usually relieved of their weapons."

"I meant before."

"Your shooter, please."

The agent said to the ceiling, "If a One wants your
gun, you have to give it to him."

Apple held out his hand laconically. "I'll mention you
in dispatches. Thanks. Off you go."

"You've got about four minutes," the agent said
drably as he went out of the cabin.

After pocketing the shells he took from the revolver,
Apple followed. Guns he had disliked—but could stand
if they were unloaded—ever since he had nearly shot
an ear off the firearms instructor at Damian House. In
addition to that, he didn't care for the noise.

Going briskly along the passage, Apple came level
with the dining saloon, where he saw the steward. The
man lay through the open door, curled up on his side as
though asleep. He was even snoring.

Apple went on.

Down a short companionway he found another victim of the spy game's toys. It was Sailor, the man who
had dragged Mimi to a car outside the Bunker.

Stepping over him, Apple went on. He was starting to
feel jittery about the time available.

That he took another stairway downward was because Linda had mentioned being on a lower level. He
came onto a passage lined with doors. Since trying each
one would eat too much time, he took a chance and
shouted, calling, "Linda!"

The response was immediate. It came from the door closest: "Here I am!"

The handle turned in his grip, the door opened to his push. Apple sidled inside with the gun held high by his chest the way they did and wearing an expression of wary toughness. He felt not jittery but marvellous.

Linda was sitting in a chair with a magazine. She asked, "Is that a gun?"

"It is," Apple said, his lips stiff. In terse sentences he explained that there was no time to lose if they wanted to get away safely. He had dealt with some of the crew but there were others around. The situation was fraught with danger.

Linda asked, "Really fraught?"

"Yes. We have to be fast."

"I'm still wearing this manacle."

"I'll carry you. Stand up."

When Apple had Linda looped across his shoulders in the fireman's lift, he found he was unable to get through the door. Not letting that spoil things for him, he thought of his Wiley and Madam X ploys during the unloading, transfer to outside and re-hoist.

Back in the present again, Apple strode along the passage and ignored that he was needing to keep his knees bent so that Linda wouldn't scrape the ceiling.

Up the companionway Apple stepped over Sailor, when Linda asked in a whisper, "Is he dead?"

In a normal tone: "Naw. I just gave him a little tap on the noggin."

"I would never have believed it."

"Mmm?"

"You're a harder man than you seem, Walter Brent."

"Oh well."

In a tingly glow like a painless blush, not caring that

Linda was faced the wrong way to see the steward—or
so he told himself once he had accepted that it would be
too difficult to make a turn by the door even if he did
manage to think of an excuse for doing so—Apple continued topside.

There, in breezy gull-cry desertion, he puts his gun
away in an inside breast pocket. The act felt sweet. Had
he been alone he might have brought the gun out for a
repeat.

He trod deck to the handrail opening. Below, at the
gangway's bottom, sat the Brit agent in a small boat
whose outboard motor was chugging reassuringly.

As Apple went carefully down the steps he said,
"Linda, meet Jenkins, my assistant." He hoped his
laboured breathing wasn't noticeable. "Jenkins, say
hello."

The two exchanged mumbles.

Apple said, "Old Jenks has a skeleton key."

"Coincidence," Linda murmured.

"No, I Morse signalled for him to bring one out with
him, you see."

"Hard and clever."

Apple said, "He'll release you while I handle the boat.
He has a talent for these itsy-bitsy things." He hoped
that the face he was pulling for the agent would convey,
*If I used Locks Five, I might give myself away as a
spook.* "That's right, isn't it, Jenks?"

The Brit's answer came out with the unnatural nasal
clack of a ventriloquist's dummy. "Yes, boss."

His legs less than mountain solid from carrying the
weight, Apple hurried to reach the gangway bottom
and to step aboard. The boat rocked. The agent said,
"Steady as she goes."

For one sickening moment Apple thought he was

about to overbalance. He could see himself and Linda
falling overboard. Next, as he weaved, he thought it was
only Linda who would land in the sea, which he saw as
infinitely worse, therefore decided that if that looked
like happening he would make himself go on in as well.
His weaving went on.

The agent said a comforting, "That's the way."

Linda asked, "Wouldn't it be better, Wally-o, if you
were to put me down?"

"Just going to do that," Apple said, quietly panting.
In a fast stoop he set her down on a seat, then, unbur-
dened, sat back himself with a bump.

"There now," the Brit said.

Through an unsteady laugh Apple said he had hated
to put his charge down so soon, she was as light as a
feather, while his mouth moved to not show his disappointment, which he failed to recognise as such, at not
being able to feel gallant to the last.

When they were moving, quickly drawing away, Apple at the tiller, the agent paused in his lock picking to
look at the yacht. He said, "Too bad."

Apple: "What?"

"That's going to make going back a bit difficult for
you."

Apple looked behind. Watching them from the deck
of the yacht was Sailor. He was holding a rifle. Apple
turned. He asked, "Why would I want to go back?"

"You forgot your hair-piece," the agent said. "Boss."

FIVE

The café, obscure, had dirty windows. It looked from outside more like one of those vacant shops that nobody wants because the rent is too low for the place to be any good. Inside there were more cats than customers, all but one of whom were dreaming over *vin ordinaire.*

Apple sat recuperating with a pot of tea. He was still unsteady from the danger. Not the possible danger of returning to get Bernard, for he had no intentions of dealing with an armed heavy, but the actual danger which had lived until, ashore, he had got Linda safely away from the agent: he, at any moment, could have created acute embarrassment by asking for his gun back.

Linda had been escorted by Apple back to her hotel. She didn't know whether or not she was going to report her curious experiences to the police, she had said, nor did she know if it would be wise to meet the alarming Walter Brent again.

"But you could try giving me a call."

"I could, couldn't I?"

"But until the auction this evening, I'll be collapsed on my bed."

Apple sipped his tea. Alarming, he mused, as he did every time his mind veered close to suggesting to him that if he were as brave as he seemed to believe, he would be on his way to rescue Bernard. Alarming. Hard.

Already Apple had pointed out to himself patiently that he could manage wondrous well without the hairy mask, since the caper had reached a hot stage. Falcon would be back from Nice with empty hands and have joined others of the team in looking for Wiley. Which, Japanese tourists being as numerous here as in any other vacation/historical spot in Europe, was not going to be easy.

Another item in his favour, Apple saw as he poured out his second cup of tea, was that Falcon & Co. might not know of the prisoners' escape. It depended on if the yacht had ship-to-shore communication. Sailor and the rest couldn't get to land without a boat, short of swimming, and it was a known fact that, oddly, seafaring folk were poor swimmers.

Therefore, Apple reckoned sunnily, with only the steward and Bullybeef having seen him void of Bernard, he was going to be fine. All he needed now was to come up with the next stage of the game.

Alarming, Apple thought. He thought it several times at intervals which he spaced shrewdly, not wanting to cripple it with familiarity, while he sipped his way through that strong second cup.

Tea finished, Apple, calm, brought out his watch and began putting it together. During the chore, he gave his mind fully to the matter of the next stage.

A possible ploy occurred to Apple as he was strapping his watch into place. It was bluff. The result could be positive if he approached every one of those who stood a chance of being Owner, including the prime suspect, and said:

"Look. I'll level with you. I'm Walter Brent. I'm here

looking for a particular manuscript, and you, I now know, have it. So let's do business."

That could nicely do the trick, Apple felt, though he did have reservations. What sounded all right in his head might come across as implausible when spoken.

Under his breath Apple mumbled a variation of the bluff. Again it sounded reasonable, and only one of the customers took any notice, giving him a look of understanding.

But Apple still wasn't satisfied. What he needed, he nodded at, was to try his bluff out on somebody, have a rehearsal. And who would suit better than the one sure innocent, Wiley?

Smiling, Apple got up. To curry favour he took his crockery with him to the counter, where he asked its crone keeper if there was a telephone he could use. She looked sad about saying yes, exhausted after lifting the instrument onto the zinc top, glad about leaving.

Wiley had mentioned the name of his hotel. While Apple was making contact he both ran through his opening phrase and added names to the list of those who would be called next, beginning with Tyrol.

"Room seventeen," the voice of Wiley said.

"Ah, good afternoon to you," Apple said, pitching his tone between friendly and businesslike. "This is Thomas Wainwright calling."

"Good afternoon to *you*, Mr. Wainwright."

"I'll come straight to the point, if I may. But no. Hold on. Before I do, I ought to start by telling you that I'm not Thomas Wainwright."

After a pause: "You just said you were. And you are. I recognise the voice."

"What I meant," Apple said, "was that I am me, yes, the man whom you know as Thomas Wainwright."

"But you're not?"

"That's right."

Wiley asked, "So who is?"

"Who is what?"

"Thomas Wainwright."

Apple was getting confused. He said persuasively, "It's just a name. I picked it out of the air. There's no such person. I used it to cover my real identity."

There was another pause. It ended with Wiley asking, his pace as slow as a dirge, "Would your real name, by any chance, happen to be Walter Brent?"

"Yes," Apple said in relief. "It certainly would."

"I knew it."

"You did?"

"Almost," Wiley said, bubbling. "I suspected it all along. It was the height, you see, and the hair. I felt sure you were the celebrated Walter Brent. You had to be."

"And you were right."

Bubbles holding: "Let us, however, not take anything for granted. To prove to my satisfaction who you are, allow me to ask you a question."

"But of course."

"How many Frisian cows are there in the herd on your Quebec property?"

Apple laughed. Partly this was to give himself time, because although he remembered being given that piece of information by Agnes or Marie, he couldn't remember what it was; partly he laughed because his answer didn't matter in the slightest, Wiley's acceptance not mattering.

Choosing the first number that slid into his head, Apple said, "One thousand nine hundred and eighty-eight."

"Correct," Wiley said. "You are undoubtedly Walter Brent."

"That's true."

"But I'll let you in on a little secret. I had no idea how many Frisians you have. I was bluffing."

"Good for you. Now look. To get to the point of—" Wiley said, "The way you responded, that confidence, answered my question better than the actual number."

"Okay. But to the purpose of this call."

"Yes. Look here, Mr. Brent—"

"Wait, please," Apple cut in. "I want to tell you that I now know—"

"Please, Mr. Brent. Later. Explanations over the Thomas Wainwright impersonation can wait."

"No, no, it's not that."

Wiley said implacably, "I have to talk to you about a serious, urgent matter."

"So have I. You see, I know that—"

"*Later*, Mr. Brent. Right now I must tell you about a certain manuscript in my possession. You might find it interesting."

With his mouth poised for speech, Apple held. When he continued it was with a quiet, "Manuscript, did you say?"

"I did. It will not, I expect, be the kind of matter with which you would normally associate yourself. You have the reputation of being a collector of refinement. However, this is special. Unique."

Apple stopped the slow nodding he had started. He asked, "Shall I guess or do you want to tell me?"

The street was busy with afternoon shoppers. In addition to that element of safety, conveniently walking in the right direction were two tallish men and an even taller woman. Apple tagged on closely behind the trio.

"We must meet," Wiley had said, excitedly in full bubble once it was established that yes, Walter Brent would be greatly interested in the essay on Sherlock Holmes written by none other than his creator, Sir Arthur Conan Doyle. "We must meet without delay."

"We must," Apple had agreed. He was being sensible even while stunned, like a boxer holding on. "But not at your hotel nor mine. I think we're both being watched."

"I have had that feeling for some time."

"Listen. Leave your hotel by the back way. If you can, change your appearance. Go discreetly to the Carlton terrace. We'll meet there."

"Isn't that rather public, Mr. Brent?"

"Somehow, I think that might be the safest," Apple had said. "I'll explain later."

At the moment, trailing along behind the tall trio, Apple was explaining to himself that obviously he had secretly suspected Wiley of being Owner, which is why he had telephoned him first.

Why he had handed Owner's identity to Falcon & Co. as a gift, unrequested at that, Apple didn't bother to try explaining because he didn't bother to recall the gifting.

At a corner the trio turned. Apple kept on, heading for the Croisette, lurking along on the inside of the pavement in a culprit stoop. And, as the palm trees came into view, he started finally to feel stimulated, understand that it looked as though he was about to actually meet with success in this strange caper.

Apple gave his back a mental straightening. Against all odds, and with skilled competition from who knew how many foreign espionage agencies, handicapped by having no clues to go on as to who had the Property, he had won through. He had escaped death and various dangers. He'd had rendezvoused with four glamorous women, some of them enemy operatives. He had resisted seduction by a naked French beauty. He had been attacked and followed, waylaid and trapped and imprisoned. But he had obtained what he had been sent out into the field to obtain. He had brought it off.

Quickly, Apple started listing the high-point moments of the Cannes caper. This was to avoid the moral query which had just surfaced, the one he had all along been vigorously suppressing: If the manuscript seemed genuine, was he going to be a party to its destruction?

Giving up on the listing trick, Apple went so far as to face tedious reality with the defence that such queries had nothing to do with rough, tough, smart, hard, successful espionage agents who had countable high-point moments.

And alarming, Apple thought.

He came to the Croisette. Turning right, he went along in front of hotels, cafés and the elegant businesses offering gowns and gems and Alfa Romeos. When he came within a sapphire's toss of the Carlton he stopped to give the place a thorough twice over.

Wiley was there already. He sat at a table on the near side of the terrace, in profile. The other tables were mostly occupied, this being the time when people were starting to think of that first drink of the day.

Apple spotted Mimi. Dressed as subduedly as a small elephant on a single roller-skate, a scarf over her cap of dark curls, she stood semi-hidden on the terrace's far edge, under the tall porch. He steady gaze was on the man in the panama hat.

Obviously, Apple reckoned, Mimi had the Oriental figured for a hot prospect as Owner and was playing bird-dog: keeping him under observation until help arrived. Which could be any minute now.

Apple moved forward. At the terrace steps he sank low and then even lower after reaching their top, finishing on his hands and knees. He began to crawl between tables.

On the whole there was little fuss over his passage. This was, after all, the Carlton, where certain people were apt to go to extraordinary lengths in order to be noticed. Apple caused a man to splutter on his martini, caused one woman to cover her knees and another to give her legs more exposure.

In raising his head along the way to check direction, Apple saw that Wiley had, in fact, made an effort toward changing his appearance. On his top lip was carefully drawn, in pencil, a hairline moustache. Proudly he stroked it with the stem of his pipe.

Apple continued his crawl. Causing on the way only a muffled shriek from a young man with dangly earrings, he circled to the rear of the Oriental's table. He arrived immediately behind Wiley and said:

"Psst. Don't look 'round. It's me."

Although Wiley twitched, he went on facing front. He whispered, "What's up?"

"You're being watched. Act normal."

"I did have the suspicion a girl was following me when I came here."

"She's waiting for reinforcements, as I see it. You have to get away from here as soon as possible."

An undertone of excitement in his voice, Wiley said, "Roger, Mr. Brent."

"We'll meet somewhere else in about an hour."

"Why so long?"

"Somehow these people got on to you, and I'll have to get them off you."

"How did they get on to me, I wonder."

"Who can tell," Apple said brusquely, impatient with the irrelevant. He craned upwards to peer over at the porch. Mimi, no amateur, was seeable from here simply as a slice of face.

Wiley was saying, "Maybe it has something to do with a photocopy that was sent to me. It was supposed to be a page from the Doyle manuscript."

"And it wasn't, of course."

"Naturally not, Mr. Brent. A very poor fake. It wouldn't fool a myopic child."

"Apart from all that," Apple said, brusque again, "where shall we meet?"

After they had agreed on a quiet bar near the railway station, Wiley asked, "Who are these followers and watchers and photocopy senders anyway?"

"People who'd like to relieve you of the manuscript by fair means or foul. I'll explain later. No time now. I hope, by the way, that you have it in a safe place."

"Never fear, Mr. Brent. I'm not so foolish as to trust it to a hotel room or even a hotel safe. It's where it has been for quite some time now—taped to my stomach."

Apple drew his breath in slowly. A reach away, he thought in awe and fear. Anyone's reach.

He said, "You've got to leave here fast. Be super-careful. As well as other dangers to you, I'm being impersonated. I have a double. So beware of imitations."

Stoutly, Wiley said, "Forewarned is forearmed."

"The next thing is," Apple said, "how to get you away from here without you being seen leaving. We don't want to have you followed."

"Simple. I'll go the way you came." He sounded like a boy who wants to join in the fun.

"If the lady sees you've gone from this table, she'll come charging over at once, before you've had the time to get clear of the area."

"Then I'd better stay here, apparently."

"I beg your pardon?"

Speaking with his head turned to one side and the corner of his mouth stretched down, Wiley said, "This is my plan, Mr. Brent. Ready?"

Feeling distantly slighted, Apple said a dry, "Ready." He scratched his ribs to show he had other interests.

"We'll switch. I'll sink from sight in a natural way, as if I've dropped something, pass you my hat and my pipe and crawl away. You're with me so far?"

Like sandpaper: "I am."

"You will get into my chair. With the hat on, your head tilted down and my pipe held before your face, you'll pass muster from a distance."

"As a matter of fact," Apple said, believing himself, "I was just about to suggest the same thing."

"Then shall we?"

"We will."

"Right, Mr. Brent," Wiley said in a leadership voice. "When I give the signal."

"I'll give it," Apple said hurriedly, adding with no measurable pause a gabbled, "One two three—go!"

Five fumbled seconds later Apple was easing himself into a low, low sit on the chair, Wiley's pipe in his hand, the panama pulled down on his brow, and hearing from nearby a muffled shriek.

Still in recovery from the annoyance of having seen that Wiley possessed plentiful hair, Apple looked over at the porch. Showing there without change was Mimi's slice of face. Elsewhere, only one or two tourists who had been watching surreptitious events from adjacent tables were undeceived by the switch. They looked away when Apple gave them each a gleaming smile.

Okay, he thought apropos the situation. All stable for the moment. Now we have to conjure up an idea for how to get the predatory pack off the heels of our man with a treasure on his belly.

So Apple started to dwell morosely on what might have been. Your real genuine rough smart hard espionage agent would not have let that treasure go, he acknowledged. He would have stuck a gun in Wiley's back or simply bashed him on the head, any move whatever, with or without finesse or pity, in order to get his hands on the manuscript. That's what your real true spook would have done.

From gazing wistfully in the direction taken by Wiley, Apple looked back at the porch. He saw that Mimi had moved out into greater prominence now that she had company. Toweringly beside her in blazer and Bernardesque headgear stood Double.

Even as Apple was getting the enemy pair in focus, they began to move, coming across.

Without obvious haste, Apple made his departure. Meerschaum pipe he slipped into a pocket, hat he put on the table as he oozed gracefully to the floor. He started to crawl, but on toes instead of knees, thus allowing for a canter pace. With no more than five metres to go, he soon made it to the bar's open French windows.

Rising as he went inside, he attracted no attention. He walked between tables toward the lobby. Beyond the windows, going the other way, were Double and

Mimi. The perfunctory glance they threw inside startled Apple until he remembered that they wouldn't recognise him even if they saw him clearly. They hadn't seen the recent yacht guest without his ensemble of wig and beard.

Reaching the lobby, Apple went out under the porch, where he took up the pitch vacated by Mimi. She and Double, he saw, were at the table, latter looking with disgust at the panama hat, former scanning around worriedly.

What became of Sickles who flopped? Apple wondered. Did they get sent to Siberia? He told himself it was not his problem. Definitely not.

Seeing his impersonator go inside the building formed a welcome diversion for Apple. Busily he explained to himself that Double would be checking the washrooms, of course, and it was the right step to take because Wiley could have gone there on a nature call if not to hide.

Apple avoided looking directly at Mimi until the return of Double. At his curt headshake her expression of worry increased. She turned and strode away.

Heart hardened, Apple watched the tall man and short woman leave the terrace, confer briefly on the pavement, set off in different directions along the Croisette. Double came this westerly way.

When he had gone by, Apple left the porch and began to follow. He walked in the gutter to reduce his height as well as keeping a score of pedestrians between himself and his imitator, who was glancing about him with an urgent manner. When he turned off the Croisette he started giving his attention to shops and doorways.

Apple found an idea for getting the pack off Wiley.

He mused: we dispose of Double, take his place by putting on the hairpiece, go to the others and tell them that Wiley has just been seen getting in a taxi and over-heard asking to be driven somewhere or another far afield.

Apple scoffed. He questioned how he could possibly be successful in passing himself off as Double to the man's close associates, which objection enabled Apple to ignore that he was discarding the idea because of that first part, disposal of his impersonator.

The man in front turned again, circling the block. Less people about, Apple dropped farther back, and then more so when he saw Mimi approaching in the distance. She, too, was peering into places where the prey could have hidden. Her hands were held together.

Due to a burst of aggressive cogitation, brought on to cower thoughts of Siberia, Apple got another idea. It was audacious and brilliant, he allowed, and probably even better than that, he further agreed, on account of his natural modesty making him view it in a lesser light.

Double and Mimi arrived at a meeting. Apple stepped into the road and set out to cross it at a lengthy obliqueness, arms on a jaunty swing. When he was drawing abreast of where stood the enemy pair, his loud footfalls brought their heads around, at which point he stopped observing them askance, looked directly across and then stopped with a jerk.

"Well!" he said, smiling but surprised, a man faced with the not unwelcome unexpected.

The pair looked at one another, looked back at Apple. He went over to them and halted with a cheerful, "What're you doing here, Mr. Wainwright?" His voice he made deeper, his Canadian accent he made more acute, his physical attitude he made different to that of Appleton Porter.

Double being as silent as his colleague, though both were staring fixedly, Apple went on, "I thought you'd be in Monte by now, Mr. Wainwright. What happened?" Not waiting for an answer, for any type of response, he turned to Mimi: "I must apologize, young lady, for this rude interruption, as well, of course, as explain it."

"That's okay," she said vaguely, in English, her eyes scrutinising his features as though looking for flaws.

"But first allow me to introduce myself," Apple said. "My name's Walter Brent."

Again the pair exchanged a look, although they kept their eyes on Apple until right at the end of the slow swivel of their heads toward one another. They turned back to him fast as he continued:

"Mr. Wainwright, here, I met earlier today, for the first time. I had just arrived in Cannes and the second thing I was told of was this guy who had been sort of impersonating me, but in a disguise." He smiled on. "It was amusing as hell, as well as flattering, but naturally I had to find out what it was all about, right?"

Mimi nodded dumbly. Double said, "Yes."

Apple gave him a wink before saying, "So I went to his hotel, the Mérimée, and we had a nice chat. It seems he thought the impersonation might help him locate an oddball manuscript supposedly written by an English novelist called Sir Arthur Conan Doyle. A forgery, of course."

Mimi looked hopeful. Double said, "Oh?"

"Curiously, the manuscript was the *first* thing I heard about this morning. I was offered it by a dealer, the one our friend here had been looking for and seemed to think was either a Frenchwoman or an Oriental. Does all this sound a little complicated, young lady?"

Mimi shook her head. So did Double.

Apple said, "The dealer left for home when he learned I wasn't interested, but I was able to give his address in Monte Carlo to Mr. Wainwright." He turned toward Double. "Did you lose it? Or maybe you've been there already. Maybe you bought the manuscript, mm?"

Neither of the pair seemed to know how to react. Apple surged on, "Ah, but you did say something about having to meet a girl first. An Australian, I think." To Mimi: "Perhaps you are she. Or perhaps I'm letting cats out of bags." He tried to look embarrassed, lowering his eyes and swaying. "Oh hell. I'd best get on my way. I talk too much. But I'll give you that address again, Mr. Wainwright, if you've lost it."

The silence that followed was broken by applause. Somebody behind Apple was clapping languidly. Mimi and Double joined in, similarly without vigour, slapping their hands together at a derisive plod.

Apple looked up and around. The rear applauder, standing some three metres away, was Bullybeef. Dropping his hands, he said, "Nice try."

Tensing for action, Apple said, "Thank you."

"How'd you get off the yacht?"

"I flew," Apple said. "Like this." He burst into a run.

The race's hectic speed lasted until they were in another street. Track the middle of the road, with Apple leading by several metres from Bullybeef, with Double that same distance back and slightly ahead of Mimi, the racers were creating a furious pace when the policewoman came into view. Her mouth pursed on a whistle, she was about to herd schoolchildren across the roadway.

One of the worst things you could do on a caper was get involved with the police, who were destructively nosy. Knowing this as thoroughly as he did, Apple had no need to order his body to slow down; it was slowing even before the woman in uniform had swung her head this way. By the time she had registered the racers, they were no longer racing.

With their positions the same, the four continued along the street, Apple giving the policewoman a debonair salute in passing. He felt fine. Being long of leg he was a good walker, he was fit, all he had to do was keep going at a steady pace and the others would gradually fall back. They daren't risk anything too drastic in public places.

Another block was covered. As all along, people turned to stare with brief curiosity. Allayingly, the three chasers wore grins, which, if he hadn't known already, would have told Apple what profession they were in, which was why he made sure he looked worried whenever he glanced back, putting his smile on again to turn front.

With more blocks covered, direction aimless, nothing happened except Double took over the lead from Bullybeef. Then Apple began to feel less fine.

In his side was the hint of a stitch, in his lungs a shadow of labouring, in his stomach a reminder that he had eaten a heavy lunch. There was also in his frame a reminder that striding a fair distance was an activity he hadn't indulged in often enough of late.

Looking behind while rounding a corner onto a busier, shop-lined street, Apple was disturbed to see that

Double, his grin on for more than just show, had closed the gap. The others were also gaining.

While explaining to himself so as not to feel offended that, naturally, full-time operatives were bound to be in better shape than a faceless one, Apple cast about for a way to win the race other than by attrition.

The street was one-way for traffic, and it wasn't going this way. There were no convenient vehicles, motorcycles or whatevers standing around in any case. The answer seemed to be Lizarding in a business place.

From the roadway Apple examined the shops on either side as he strode. He was trying to ignore the increase in his stitch and labouring of lungs. His smile was growing equally painful.

He saw a store that would serve: its doorway was open and free of people. Slipping between parked cars, he crossed the pavement, went inside, reduced his stride to a brisk walk to go along an aisle.

The store was for women, selling clothing and accessories, with counters high and low between the half-dozen aisles, which were bowling-alley long.

Apple, who had noted already the attention brought by his male presence and purposeful walk, looked back as he neared the store's rear. The trio were coming at an implacable march, grins in bloom.

To the right in the back wall was a door marked EXIT, Apple saw on facing front. He made a gesture toward it one second before grabbing off a counter two handfuls of flimsy nightgowns, which he threw aloft directly above his head. They were floating down behind him as he reached the aisle's end, where, crouching, he turned left.

A shopper gaspingly drew her skirt to her knees as though the bulk passing below were a flock of mice; a woman in the staff smock said, mysteriously, that he ought to ask the cleaners; and then Apple was midway down the next aisle. He was not being followed.

Unable to resist, while still moving he straightened far enough upward to see over the counter top. Gratifyingly, his ruse had worked. The enemy trio had gone to, were standing by, the exit door. But it seemed to be locked.

Apple wasn't quick enough. When Mimi's eyes, roving around the store while her colleagues gave the door their attention, swept in the direction of his head, Apple had been drained of too much snap to get out of sight in time. He heard Mimi call to the others.

Rising to full height, he ran. His shoes thundered on the wooden floor. Assuring himself that those camps in Siberia couldn't possibly be as bad as people said (anti-Communist propaganda was so vicious), he reached the store's entrance and passed outside.

The supply of pedestrians on the pavement being as much a hindrance to those behind him as to himself, Apple stayed there to continue his progress, which he had reduced to a medium, manageable pace on account of those same sauntering pedestrians.

Not until the second corner did Apple look behind. The trio were coming strongly, their grins as showy, their order the same as before: Double well in front of a lumbering Bullybeef who was leading Mimi by a short head.

That one or more of his chasers lacked the extra energy to come abreast on the roadway, head him off, was a consolation to Apple. It alleviated the ache he felt at not being able to bring himself to create obstacles, pull people around behind him into the trio's path.

Apple slogged on along another street. His stitch was

like a poking finger with a horny nail, his lungs had
shrunk, his body felt as if it had been left out all night.

When yet another corner had been turned, the farm-
produce market soared into view. It was a collection of
individual stalls under a high, high roof with pillar sup-
ports. Late now, only one double row of stalls was in
use, with the farmerish attendants yelling prices at
each other where there were no people going by between, which meant in most places.

Apple crossed the road, speed dropping, spirits rising. Here were useable obstacles aplenty. Just so long as
the chasers were sheepesque enough to follow him into
the two-metre-wide lane between stalls.

They were. At the same trot as Apple had changed
down to, Double and Bullybeef and Mimi followed on
as faithfully as the converted. Not until the panting girl
had come into the lane did Apple start.

Zagging rapidly from side to side, he flung produce
down behind him. There were cabbages, melons and
various fruits. There were coconuts, peppers and leeks.
There were bunches of bananas and sacklets of spuds.
Unconsciously, Apple sought to select a nice variety.

After a hiatus of surprise, the stallholders began to
shout. They also shook battle fists, Apple saw on looking
back to check results and finding them good, the trio
being made to trip and skip.

He continued his rapine, trailing shouted curses. He
would have hummed at the awful glory of destruction,
worrying about himself later, had he not been conscious of the fact that he was undermining these market
people's livelihood.

Almost as strong was his discomfort at the mess he
was instigating. Another look behind showed him that
what Double trod on was further mashed by Bullybeef

and then irrevocably splattered by Mimi. But he went on plundering with vigour, callous as a wall.

While slapping produce one-handed off stalls at either side, Apple looked ahead, making selections. He noted that all the other marketeers had become aware of the attack and of its approach. Some were crawling protectively onto their stalls, some were winding up their throwing arms to defend with fruit missiles.

An orange whizzed past Apple's head. Glancing back to see if it had scored on the chasers, he noted that the underfoot squelch was starting to have an effect on the girl. Arms aloft, she skidded and weaved like a tightrope walker on slack string.

When Apple looked behind again a moment later he saw that Mimi had succumbed. She lay on her back as if dazed. One down and two to go, Apple thought.

He jogged zaggingly on. He detoured a bemused shopper, dodged a pineapple missile, flung down behind him a stack of lettuces, three cauliflowers and one lost grape.

He was nearing the lane's end. On its right, alone, stood the last stall. Its keeper was a hurt-looking man in a wheelchair, one leg stuck out horizontal in a plaster cast.

Although there were obstacles galore on the stall, Apple couldn't make himself use them. After he had hesitated fractionally by a tempting pyramid of oranges, he began to run on. At once the man started to bellow, the gist being that he shouldn't be spared the plunder because the other marketeers would then hate him.

Shunting his chair forward angrily, the man snarled, "Do something, you bastard."

Apple was already past. Semi-reversing in discom-

fort, he watched as Double scraped by in front of the
wheelchair, and next as it was hit full on by Bullybeef,
who, with a yell, crashed over it. One of his flailing arms
sent the oranges bursting from their pile before he
landed on his head.

Two down and one to go, Apple mused as he went on.
He needed the confidence of that to make himself build
up speed again: his physical despair had grown. He
knew he couldn't keep going much longer.

Back on a street, Apple stayed alert for transport,
although he knew it was unlikely he would have the
time for acquisition before Double caught up, followed
eventually by the other two.

"Mr. Wainwright!"

The call came not from behind but ahead; from a big
man in an Alpine hat. After his call, Tyrol began to run
forward, his arms spread in welcome.

There was a convenient alley. Apple, head down,
breathing like a fiction rapist, went into it at a running
trudge. He looked back.

Surprisingly, Tyrol had not followed. He had slowed
by the alley's mouth, jittering about on spread feet like
a fevered goalkeeper and still looking the way he had
been going when he called out.

Into view pounded Double. Just as he was about to
turn into the alley, he was grabbed by Tyrol, who said a
nasty, "Gotcha."

Not waiting to see any more, not even bothering to
think three down and none to go, Apple slogged on.

It was the waiting room of a chiropodist. The walls
had lurid charts and cool diplomas, the chairs held
three people. These were a pair of fat men with offended expressions, and Apple, who, due to the fact

that he was finally at rest, wore a face of cautious bliss, which could have been why the fat men looked offended.

Minutes ago, the peak of his corporal distress abating, Apple had pushed through the door of the entryway he was sagging in as it came to him that pursuit could be fast: either Double getting rid of Tyrol or Tyrol getting rid of Double on seeing he had grabbed an impostor.

Inside, a nurse had shown Apple into the waiting-room with a pale smile in answer to his statement that he just wanted them scraped at the back.

Recovered from his embarrassment at discovering (from wall-charts) that it was not a dentist's he was in, Apple drooped in the luxury of being unmobile.

The inner Apple was different. He stood upright to receive medals: one rewarding his brilliance in getting away from the chasers, one in recognition of his establishing that Bullybeef and Tyrol were not, after all, on the same team, and one for his not having a single sear of guilt over the destroyed market produce.

Feeling very much the cynical pro, Apple at last gave his mind to the next move, once he had sneaked away from here, before getting called in to see the doctor.

Since there was quite a while to go until his rendezvous with Wiley, Apple mused, he would try the Oriental's hotel to see if he was there, and maybe stop on the way at a post office to buy a money order that he could send to a local charity in the name of the stallholders, and later go back to that last stall to . . .

Annoyed, Apple kicked himself, literally, slapping his right foot against his left. The fat men gasped, the while leaning back and easing their feet off the floor. Apple mumbled an apology for disturbing the silence.

But he decided he had had his fill lately of eccentrics.

Also if he were to leave now, before being recuperated in full from his marathoning, it would punish him for having slipped into that juvenile sentimentality in respect of the marketeers.

Getting up, sorry nevertheless about that loutish silence-breaking, Apple went on tip toe into the outer office, where the nurse turned to look at him with stiff, wary eyes and a backwards slope.

As he reversed out to the street, Apple told her that the problem was solved. He had just discovered that this morning by accident he had put pepper in his socks instead of the usual athlete's-foot powder. Now he was going home to rectify matters.

His inner man accepting another medal for the adroit improvisation, Apple sidled along beside the buildings. It was five blocks to Wiley's hotel going in this direction, three blocks in the other, and as he couldn't claim to be in need of exercise to explain why he wasn't shortcutting past the post office, which he wasn't thinking about, Apple acknowledged that he wanted time to plan how he was going to bargain for the Property.

Since Apple had never bargained for anything in his life, not least that someday he would become a part-time espionage operative, his planning took five seconds. When Wiley named a price, he would say, "Okay."

Pleased by this pragmatic advancement, Apple hurried on his way.

Soon he came within sight of the Oriental's hotel, above whose entrance dangled the flags of many nations. It was in turning his eyes sharply from these to cancel the fact that he had been seeking, and been prepared to be irked at the absence of, the Union Jack, as well as to pretend that such a patriotic commonplace was beyond him, that Apple saw one of the Competition. He halted.

It was Denver Campbell. The pale Scot in sickly tweed was sitting among a dozen other people at a sidewalk café across the street from the hotel. Seemingly, he was reading a newspaper. Apple, however, could give that the lie, having learned in Training Seven all about head angles. Denver Campbell was keeping a watch on the flag-topped entrance.

Apple, on the café side of the street, slipped up marble steps into an office building's wide recessed entry. If he were seen by Campbell, he reckoned, the height alone would give him away, despite being Bernardless. He would do a spot of watching himself.

But why was Campbell doing it? Apple queried. Was he on to Wiley as Owner? Had Wiley been dropping hints?

That last Apple dismissed as ridiculous. The Oriental, he pointed out, was far too cautious and shrewd . . . and it wasn't simply a matter of the money involved, it was the wastage, all that edible food going—

Slapping one foot against the other, Apple nodded over the reminder of how smart he had been here. Not charging directly into the hotel, he had given the scene a careful panning first. It paid to stay alert.

Another pay-off came twenty minutes later. With the scene unchanged, Apple, on the verge of leaving for his date, did a double-take on a woman approaching the hotel.

She wore large sunglasses, a head scarf tied under the chin, a baggy raincoat of a forgettable shade. What it was about her that struck a familiar chord with him, Apple didn't know, unless it was her walk.

She entered the hotel. When she came out again, so
quickly that she was still on Apple's mind, she caught
sight of him and stopped in a teeter. He nodded in
friendly fashion so as not to hurt her feelings, but then
tensed up as he realised she could be one of the Sickles.

With a no-nonsense settling of her sunglasses, the
woman came firmly across the street toward him. On
looking back at her after a glance toward Denver
Campbell, who was showing no interest, Apple relaxed,
in respect of danger if not doubtful possibilities. He had
recognized the woman as Linda.

She came up the steps. "Yes, sport," she said like a
sentence of death. "Very neat."

"I beg your pardon?"

"You set a neat trap and I fell for it."

"Yes?"

"Now you know my game."

"Sure."

"You're nobody's fool, Mr. Walter Brent."

"Oh?"

"But I reckon that innocent facade fools most people," Linda said.

Apple said understandingly, though not understanding what she was talking about, "You mustn't blame
yourself."

"Well, I did think it odd when you gave out so freely
with information over lunch. I didn't suspect, though,
that you were baiting a trap for me, to find out what I
was up to, when you told about the Oriental who had
the goods you were after."

"And you're after too?"

"Obviously," Linda said, less cold. She went into a
grumble about all the checking she had been doing, the

while in disguise to stay free of the Falcon team. "With no result. And all for a lie."

"No, it wasn't," Apple said before he could brake himself. He had been partly absent, musing, now he knew the score, that quite possibly his undermind had seen the trap value in addition to the red-herring aspect.

He amended, "I mean, yes, it wasn't true."

Linda smiled. "You're nice, Wally-o. Did anyone ever tell you you're a lousy liar?"

"I'm afraid so."

"But thanks for the info."

"It isn't going to do you any good," Apple said. "The deal's practically finalised."

"Meaning your offer can't be topped? Listen, I'm working for some of the wealthiest men in Australia— the members of FOSH. That's the Friends of Sherlock Holmes."

"And you're not a reporter?"

"I'm a private enquiry agent," Linda said, raising her sunglasses briefly as though to show a new person. "Or an eye, if you like. A good one. I usually get what I set out to get."

Apologetically Apple said, "You can't expect to win 'em all, Linda. This one belongs to me. I've set my heart on that manuscript."

"And I've set my heart on the fab bonus I'll earn for bringing home the bacon."

Apple looked at his watch. "We could get together later and argue about hearts and desires."

"What's your hurry, Wally-o?"

"I have to go meet a guy who's got the manuscript glued to him."

"Ask a silly question," Linda said, veering coolish. "If

you want to see me later, you know where I can be found. So long, rival."

That Linda went off in the one direction forced on him a choice of the other, Apple acknowledged, even though it meant passing the post office, which he could do, pass, with the greatest of ease, being an alarming, hard man of neat traps and quick thinking.

When he came out to the street from having mailed the money order, Apple saw Linda again. She was some way ahead, in the direction he had been taking, looking around like a golfer who is about to foot his ball out of the rough.

Adroitly, Linda had followed him after playing it palely indifferent, Apple saw; but, less than brilliantly, she had lost him.

While in the post office Apple had kept his mind occupied by considering the news of Linda's professional involvement. It made her even more attractive than before.

Dwelling on that again now, Apple took back that snide thought of her tailing loss being unbrilliant. She was not, he explained, used to dealing with pros at the game of hare-and-hounds, and, when he had perhaps by instinct realised he had a tail, he had easily given her the slip by side-stepping into the post office. He had even found something to do while in there.

Apple walked on in the other direction, humming.

After stopping twice on the way to ensure he wasn't being followed, and once to avoid being seen by Bully-beef, who had a piece of sticking plaster on his brow, Apple came to the rendezvous bar. He went in.

Early evening had drawn a goodly crowd, all male, all wearing work clothes and smelling of honest toil, which is less attractive than the smell of villainy on account of the licit having no mystery. Apple didn't mind.

Being tall, he had no trouble spotting the short Oriental, who was standing at the counter wearing an RAF-style false moustache and a red baseball cap. The cap was on crooked, and the length of fluffy brown hair was lower at one end than at the other.

Apple worked his way over to the bar. He said, "Sorry I'm a bit late."

Wiley looked up at him starkly. "You are mistaken, sir," he said.

"No, but it's only a few minutes."

"To repeat, sir, you are mistaken."

"What?"

"You don't know me."

Tactful, Apple told him, "Yes, the disguise is excellent. It took me a second or two, but I finally recognised you."

"You don't know me and I don't know you," Wiley said. "Do please stop molesting me or I shall call the management."

"Molesting you?"

"Who are you, sir?"

Apple patted himself on the chest. "It's me. Thomas Wainwright or Walter Brent. Have we had a drink too many?"

The Oriental began to nod knowingly. "Of course. I see now. Yes. I was warned about you."

"This is getting strange."

"You, sir, are an impostor."

Apple started nodding as the other man's nods stopped. He realised that earlier, on the Carlton terrace, he hadn't been seen innocent of Bernard by Wiley, who had not looked around while sitting at the table, nor aside while getting down to all fours.

"No no," Apple said, stabbing ten fingers on his chest. *"I'm* Brent. *I'm* the one who warned you."

"That's a good angle," Wiley said. "Top marks. But you must excuse me." Ducking around a customer, he rumpled off along the bar.

Apple had less success at the same duck. The brawny customer with more tattoos than teeth, he didn't take kindly to having his drinking arm jogged, particularly when beer slopped, enough to moisten a postage stamp.

However, by the time Apple had finished with conciliatory gabble, earned the man's miffed nod and left him with a hefty slap of friendship on the wrong shoulder, he had thought of a solution to this minor set-back.

Reaching Wiley, he said, "Maybe *you're* an impostor. That disguise is a bit too good to be true."

"Honestly?"

"If you're really the man I've arranged to meet here, you'll know if you've ever seen me before without my false hair and beard."

"I will and I haven't," Wiley said, warming like the wanted. "And there *is* something familiar about your voice."

"Thanks. And for my part, I now accept you as you. It's that cap, it makes all the difference."

"Cap," Wiley said. "Where's my hat?"

Apple said, "Left it on the table at the Carlton. Sorry. But I still have this." He brought out the meerschaum pipe. "Your ruse, by the by, worked like white magic."

"What are you drinking, Mr. Brent?"

Soon they were clinking glasses together in a toast of confusion to their enemies. Apple had his favourite

drink, sherry on the rocks, which, he knew, he de-
served for so shrewdly bringing about the set-back's
defeat. The pipe as doubt-remover he had forgotten.

"All right," Apple said. "Let's get down to business.
There's the question of money."

"Indeed there is."

"How much, in fine, were you going to ask for the
Conan Doyle manuscript?"

Wiley shook his head. "Mr. Brent," he said, speaking
earnestly, which turned his crooked moustache from
silly to poignant, "the manuscript is not for sale."

Apple asked acutely, "What's that?"

"I have decided against selling."

"Wait a minute."

Wiley said, "I am going to give it to you."

Apple was slow with his, "Eh?"

"That's right, Mr. Brent."

"Give it to me?"

"Gratis and free," Wiley said. "Without charge, rate,
fee, payment or any manner of compensation."

Apple managed, "I don't know what to say."

"Almost."

"What?"

"I do ask for one thing in return, Mr. Brent. Which is
that the manuscript not be exploited in any way. It
must not be published, reviewed, written about, talked
about, seen in a bad light, ushered in any form into the
public domain. Mr. Sherlock Holmes must not be
brought to low esteem."

"No," Apple said, thrilled by his burgeoning success.
"He mustn't." Sagging on the bar, he got impossible
flash forwards, scenes featuring himself and Angus
Watkin. In one he was strolling into Watkin's office with
the manuscript and a casual, "I convinced Owner he

should let me have it for nothing." In the other he was saying on the telephone, "Owner and I have agreed on one million pounds, which he'd like in cash."

The flash forwards were impossible because, in one, Apple didn't know where to find Watkin's office; in two, he began to blush even at the thought that he could get such an outrageous notion, and when he blushed he found difficulty in speaking, therefore would be unable to conclude the swindle. His blush was caused partly by pride.

"Mr. Sherlock Holmes is the only hero I have left," Wiley was saying. "I want to leave his reputation in younger, safer hands. I would be a nervous wreck in any case, trying to keep the manuscript safe, not being able to afford top security. You see?"

Apple said, "I see." His blush was in retreat.

Wiley said, "You are my choice as the new proprietor, Mr. Brent, since, being wealthy, you can both afford good security and have no need to make profit." He wriggled to a tallness, his voice rising with it. "You will guard this manuscript from the rabble. You will ensure that it is read only by serious Holmesian scholars. You will be ever conscious of your sacred mission."

"I will, I will," Apple said. He spoke fervently, forgetting for the moment that he was not Walter Brent, billionaire, and that Angus Watkin's plans for the Property went in quite a different direction.

"You promise?"

"I swear it."

Wiley, blinking slowly, patted Apple's arm. "You are a decent fellow, Mr. Brent."

Apple stopped forgetting. Averting his gaze he murmured, "Oh well."

"Really true blue, Mr. Brent."

"Oh, I don't know."

"I trust you implicitly."

Apple mumbled that he would try to do the right thing.

Wiley said, "I can see you are thinking differently already. It will be quite a responsibility."

Apple straightened. Voice up and hard, he said, "Your moustache is crooked."

Wily imbalanced it the other way. "Thank you."

"Now, let's get to the bottom line, shall we?"

"Yes, the manuscript itself. Good. I have been dying to tell you about my adventure."

Patient and cold, Apple listened.

Wiley had suspected he was being followed (his description of one of the hounds fitted Tilda), and when the enemy was closing in he had slipped into the Gallerie Centrale. On leaving again, it was by a rear door, after which he had bought his disguise and come by taxi to the bar.

As he told his tale, Wiley's eyes grew comparatively wide and he panted. He managed to look both surprised at and impressed with himself while also looking as though he didn't believe a word of it.

"I suppose you could call it inspiration," Wiley finished, reluctantly calming.

"Cap and moustache?"

"No no, Mr. Brent. Seeing how I could guarantee intermediate safety for the manuscript by nipping into the Gallerie Centrale. After all, they might have cornered me later, those people."

"True."

"What could be better than armed guards and all the other security measures already in vogue for those other valuable items in there?"

Apple began to feel worried. He asked, "What, please, is the Gallerie Centrale?"

"I thought you knew," Wiley said. "It's an auction establishment. Cleverly, I entered the manuscript for this evening's auction."

Apple stared sadly. "You cleverly . . . ?"

"No one can touch it, not even me, until after the sale is over. The officials don't know what I entered, of course. I told them it was an essay on Edgar Allen Poe."

At a run Apple said, "Which will attract bids even though no one learns what it really is which is bound to happen once the officials who are expert in this field start looking at this manuscript that every visitor to Cannes is aware of and word will spread like confetti in a wind."

Apple drew in air sharply. "What reserve did you put on it?"

Wiley said, "Reserve?"

SIX

Apple had chosen the café not for its lurky location down a flight of steps but because of it being English. This state was proclaimed outside by photographs of London landmarks and signs welcoming English tourists, inside by a waitress with Devonshire's cream complexion and cider accent. The finest in English cuisine was promised.

While a patriot, Apple gravely doubted if such a thing as English cuisine existed, and knew that even if it did, he wouldn't be all that interested. His purpose in descending to John Bull's Pantry was to avoid deepening his gloom with disappointment. Since he seemed destined in Cannes to be thwarted in his desire to have a French meal, he would turn the tables trimly on that by not trying; by, in fact, opting for a meal which originated in the core of England.

By the time he had finished the Scotch broth, Apple had stopped giving the waitress looks of reproach. When he had eaten the Welsh rarebit, he vehemently no longer recalled his pre-broth thoughts of two being able to play at the thwarting game. Over the Irish stew his sole musing in respect of matters national was that as tradition said the British lost every battle but the last, Agent One could only come out victorious from what lay ahead.

Whatever that might be. Apple knew nothing. Apart

from his feeling that this, surely, was the final round, he had no notion of what to expect when the Gallerie Centrale opened its iron doors in thirty minutes time. So Apple didn't think ahead, except as an abstraction called Victory.

He lost his gloom. He told himself he ought to have known he would do the right thing, choose such a place as John Bull's Pantry in order to have a meal of no-nonsense victuals. He decided to leave a twelve and a half percent tip. He thought of Wiley in kinder terms.

Apple had left the Oriental after realising that, for the present, there was nothing to be done retriev-ingwise about the manuscript, which would be available to its old or new owner only when the whole auction was concluded. Wiley, refusing to see the situation as difficult, had gone off to change his appearance once more: "I am becoming, one could say, a master of disguise."

Remembering that, Apple again felt gloomy. He pushed away the rest of his stew and mused indifferently that five percent would be fair as a tip when he paid the check.

Apple perked. That, he acknowledged, was a powerful sign of his professionalism as an operative. So soundly had he gone into his cover role that even in thought he hadn't used the British term "bill" but the North American "check." He was getting there in the spook business. Slowly yet surely he was getting there.

Apple sat straighter. Affably he looked at the other diners, willing to exchange nods. The three silent tourist couples at separate tables avoided his eyes as thoroughly as if they thought he might do something awful.

Couldn't blame 'em, Apple forgave. What person of sense in a foreign port would want to risk getting involved with a mysterious stranger who had a bulge under one armpit?

When one of the men glanced across, Apple looked away. He patted his stomach and told himself not to forget to leave a decent tip, perhaps fifteen percent.

Apple hummed as he continued to dwell on Victory, which brought to mind the flagship of that name at the Battle of Trafalgar, which led to recalling that Nelson's second-in-command had been claimed as a forebear by Oliver Hardy of the comedy duo Laurel and Hardy, which produced the admiral's legendary dying words, which reminded that, although victorious, he had, indeed, died.

Apple felt the approach of gloom. With a glance at his watch, he called in a murmur for the bill. He supposed he had better leave a gratuity, and expected that six or seven percent would be acceptable.

Cream and Cider came with the folded paper on a plate. Searching his face, clasping her hands, she said anxiously that she hoped he had enjoyed the meal. With his teeth on show, Apple said he had, he sure had, he could never hide his regret when it was time to leave a cozy restaurant. The waitress went away contented, backing off with bows on account of the added twenty percent.

Apple felt rich. That made him feel happy, he being no different from your man in the street who refuses to believe that wealth and happiness don't go together because if he does he will feel disloyal to his conditioning, and as that conditioning had been created mainly by his parents, there is no way he can get out of feeling happy if he feels rich, unless he comes from a family wealthy or obnoxious, which Apple did not. Apple felt happy.

This lasted until he reached the last corner before coming to the small square in which stood the Gallerie Centrale, when he began to hear the crowd's noise.

To make a reasonably accurate estimate of crowd strength at speed, started Training Nine's lesson, you counted heads in an outer one tenth of the mass.

When Apple had finished multiplying his headcount by ten, he arrived at two hundred and twenty. Not, he agreed, that it mattered how many there were, drop or add a hundred. But the arithmetic gave him something to do while he recovered from his surprise, accepted that admission to the Centrale was the reason for the mob's presence, grew a tinge accustomed to its component parts.

It was a weird crowd. Many of the people Apple had seen before over the past days, others were new, all were unrelated to Mr. and Mrs. Average.

The most ordinary-looking person in sight was a dowdy matron, who could have passed as a village schoolteacher except for the ten-inch cigar she was smoking.

For the rest, they had every kind of oddity of dress and curiosity of hairstyle, from riding britches to capes, from white Afro on an old man to a woman's combination of crew cut and ponytail. There were middle-aged male triplets in identical clothes, women whose headgear made Hattie look subdued, a tall man wearing a top hat and two pairs of spectacles, some fool in a yellow wig and a pipe with . . .

After shaking his head at Wiley, but grateful for having been made to feel superior, Apple checked out the Competition. Everyone known to him was there, spaced around the crowd's edges and in the best spycraft manner scanning about without seeming to do so.

Although safe here, peering around the corner, Apple knew he would be spotted at once were he to enter the square, and enter he had to in order to be among the first to go in the Gallerie Centrale when those big double doors opened (any minute now) so he could implement whatever plan it was that was bound to occur to him.

People were still arriving, entering the square from its other corners as well as from behind Apple. Almost, he tagged on at the back of a passing group, tweedy women in semi-deerstalker hats who were saying it was sure to be a forgery. He reckoned, however, that with him presenting a strangely normal appearance, the women might veer off into singles out of wariness.

There was a rash of timepiece-checking. It swept around the square from person to person like yawns at a party. Apple, growing nervous, turned away.

Quickly he went to the first alley, into it and along to the midway point and through a doorway without knocking. He meant business.

The room he was in was for stock, that of a shoestore. A salesgirl stood high on a ladder. She had charming legs, Apple told her in Manx as he swept by, pinking but mildly at his cheekiness.

He came into the store proper, which was closing for the day, manager bowing out a last customer with her white boxes. Crossing swiftly to the door, Apple slipped by with, "I'll wait in the car," which the man would take as meant for the woman and the woman think was meant for the man, Apple expected, not bothering with details such as the manager wondering how his customer's companion had got on the premises unseen.

At the front of the store's inset entrance a pair of teenagers were standing. Patent locals, they were discussing this strange gathering of strange people, Apple heard as he came up behind them in a crouch, which he maintained in using them as cover.

He didn't straighten when manager and customer came abreast, looking at him curiously between giving one another reassuring glances. They then noticed the congregation out front.

"What's this?" the man asked, offended.

One of the teenagers said, "Book cranks. They're waiting for the Centrale's doors to open."

"Which," the other said, "is going to happen right now, because I just saw the lights go on inside."

Apple's boost at this he helped a step higher by allowing himself to admire his honesty in musing followingly *How lucky* rather than *Neat bit of eavesdropping*.

Taking long strides with bent legs, though keeping his upper body erect, Apple swooped into the loose crowd. Familiar almost to the level of contempt with this physical gambit, he went smoothly, presenting a normal picture to all except those who were close enough to see the angled knees.

Farther and better, the implacable nature of his swoop attracted sheep, so that by the time he was halfway across the square he had collected followers, who formed additional camouflage.

The forward movement became general when, with Apple and his retinue nearly on Gallerie Centrale's fronting pavement, the iron double-doors swung inward. Hurrying, Apple was one of the first inside.

The auction room was like a small theatre without seats. Its floor sloped down from the back to a stagelike platform, on the right end of which stood the auctioneer's lectern, with centrally a bare table, where, Apple guessed, each item would be placed as it came up for sale.

He had the room sized up and was standing small near the lectern when people stopped pushing in, settled. It was a close-set crowd divided down the middle by a natural aisle which an older security guard was managing to maintain by giving pitiable coughs.

Subtlety, Apple mused. What if he sought out the auctioneer and told him that the Competition's members, each one described, were penniless or insane and should be ignored if they made a bid on anything?

But it was too late, for the auctioneer had appeared behind his lectern, which made Apple's idea seem resplendent. He swung his arm and tutted.

The crowd's mumble rose. With it rose the tension that had been lurking in smaller degree outside. The ambience started to crackle with the energy created by those passions which had brought here so many buyers and gawpers, reporters and sellers, scholars and spies: the potency of ego, the power of avarice, the lust for glory, the brutal fire of chauvinism and the bullied flame of love.

With a tap of his hammer the auctioneer, a gaunt man of quick brown foxy eyes, began giving what Apple assumed to be a standard statement on the rules in respect of bidding and buying at auction.

Nobody listened, to judge by the noise, except Apple. He only did so out of philological interest once the man, having finished his spiel in French, started a repeat in English.

As well as listening, Apple began to straighten so he could see clearly. To a professional such as himself it wasn't enough merely to hear how a person spoke a foreign language, he needed to see if the face matched.

He was pleased to note that the auctioneer's immaculate English came, correctly, from a mouth as vivacious as a hole in a rock. Apple's next note, as he looked around while sinking, gave him less pleasure. He had been seen by Bullybeef.

The heavy, his piece of sticking-plaster peeling lewdly at one end, glared triumphantly across from the middle section; glared, nodded, began to come forward.

In a circumstance like this, Apple knew, there was only one way to go. Since hounds expected hares to flee, you did the reverse, went toward instead of away from.

Setting off for the crowd's centre, crouched low, Apple was grateful that he wasn't known to the Competition as an operative. All spies of whatever nationality had similar training, which, Apple often avoided thinking, made the whole game fairly stupid at field level.

Aware of crowd movement coming from the right ahead, Bullybeef-caused eddies, Apple veered to the left. Those he slunk by looked down at him either with indifference or sympathy (but not surprise), depending on whether he met the gaze with blank eyes or with features expressing the pain created by his infirmity.

The auctioneer, having done with English, was repeating himself in German as Apple safely passed Bullybeef, had returned to his own language when Apple neared the middle section, and was talking about the sale's first item as Apple settled in a spot one person away from the aisle.

Some seconds passed before Apple, busy checking with sneaky peers that Bullybeef was over at the side, realised that the crowd, rather than quieting following preliminaries, had become much louder.

This, he soon gathered, was because of a lack of interest in the first item, a letter, which had appeared on the platform table, behind which now stood two armed guards.

The auctioneer tapped with his hammer. It made no difference, the crowd yammered on. He stopped tapping, pounded. It served only to cause a further rise in the clamour. His hammer set aside, the man appealed silently with spread arms. Among the noise could be heard whines of derision.

Not until the auctioneer started to nod as though in a lead hat did the crowd lower its seeth. He said, with reasonable peace obtained, that due to popular suggestion the first item to go on sale would be the last entered, a manuscript which seemed to have created an unusual amount of interest.

From the crowd came a sound like breathing out after a deep inhale of ozone.

"It is a manuscript unauthenticated and with no guarantees," the auctioneer said with a hint of spite. "It purports to be an essay on his craft by Edgar Allan Poe, and is offered by a Mr. Lloyd."

Apple wondered how many people here would fail to see that Lloyd spoken backwards had the sound of Doyle. Two? Three? He sighed at Wiley's wiliness.

Onto the platform came a girl with a blue folder, which she left in place of the letter. Although the crowd was maintaining its peace, the atmosphere had grown more tense. The two guards exchanged puzzled glances.

Following a tap of his hammer, the auctioneer asked,

"Would somebody care to start us off with a bid on this item which has no reserve?"

A voice called, "One million francs."

"I am offered one million," the auctioneer said, his tone changing to a chant, his eyes on the skip and dart.

A voice that Apple recognised instantly as belonging to Wiley rang out with, "One and a half million."

Oddly, since people in his profession usually have twenty-twenty auditory power, the auctioneer seemed not to hear. He asked, "Any advance on one million francs, ladies and gentlemen?"

Apple yelled almost involuntarily, "One and a half million!"

The man at the lectern looked at him, looked away, said, "Come along now, who will offer me more than one million francs?"

"One and a quarter million," someone called, getting from the auctioneer a nod and, "I am bid a million and a quarter francs for—"

"One and a half million," another voice said.

Another called, "Two million francs."

"I have a bid of two million," the man with the hammer said.

Somebody, Apple realised coldly, had stolen his resplendent idea. Somebody had warned the auctioneer that it would be pointless to take bids from certain people in the crowd. Some bloody body had no doubt fingered everyone who belonged to his own Competition.

"Two and a quarter million," called a young female voice with an Australian accent.

The auctioneer chanted, "I am offered two and a quarter million francs."

As the bidding went on, its pace more determined than hectic, Apple stopped feeling annoyed at the theft and decided on positive action. He needed to make a direct move. It was the one sure way to win.

The plan came to him at once, which, Apple willingly admitted, was on account of it being the only one available. He would run down the aisle to the front, leap onto the platform, grab the manuscript, run into the wings and look for the rear exit which, because of Wiley, he knew existed.

Except, Apple thought, that the guards would be alerted by his dash and leap. Therefore what he had to have was a diversion to keep both them unsuspicious and the crowd placid while he *walked* along the aisle to the front and then to the platform end opposite the lectern and next up the steps there and last to the table.

With his left hand he would push guard one, who would fall into guard two, grab up in his other hand the folder and run on, in the same direction.

Good pro stuff, Apple accepted, at the same time giving a mental salute of approval to his ploy of getting himself located here in the middle. Now he needed to think of a good diversion.

A man called out, "Seven million."

Another topped, "Seven and a half."

The loudest voice came when the bidding had just hit eleven million: "Don't anybody move!"

The crowd hissed, losing its murmur of talk.

"Don't anybody move!" Apple shouted again. The better to be seen, he was standing in, for him, a strange stance: on the tips of his toes. Also, he was smiling as he looked around. He didn't want to start a panic.

There was no sign of one. The crowd was as silent and still as a wet grave. Everyone stared at the speaker.

And everyone stared.

Apple tensed. Never in his life had he been the centre of so much attention, even casual attention, and this was far from casual. Two or three hundred pairs of eyes bored at him as if he were showing every flaw, revealing his every sick secret.

At the lurch he felt in his lower chest Apple caught his breath. A blush was beginning. It blossomed. It climbed at speed and claimed his head. He couldn't move, couldn't speak, could hardly think.

Weaving slightly on his toes, still wearing a form of smile, Apple stared with ghastly eyes into space and suffered this grade-one scorcher, a rarely-experienced Royal Flush.

Apple was not totally without defence. For crises such as the present he was always armed with a cerebral antidote. These, bought via newspaper advertisements, were good for two or three outings before losing their power due to familiarity. The latest, highly efficient, had been used only once. Trouble was, Apple could not at this moment remember it.

Although the crowd stared on as fixedly as ever, the silence had grown less severe. There were murmurs. There were whisperings. There were titters.

Apple, burning bright, his insteps aching, worked speech muscles to see if he could produce his diversion, tell of the escaped serpent that was perfectly harmless just so long as no one made a sudden move. He got out not a single word.

Above the low voice of the crowd could now be heard a different sound. It was the drum of footfalls on the floorboards. Apple, stifling head kept still, turned his eyes in the sound's direction.

Down the side of the room a man was moving. He

reached the steps. On climbing to the platform he became recognisable to Apple as Denver Campbell.

At a quiet pace, tugging self-consciously at his worn tweed suit, the Scot went toward the table. With one stride left to go he abrupted into action.

Mightily he shoved the nearest guard, who collapsed against his colleague, who lost his balance. Neither had yet hit the floor before Denver Campbell had snatched up the blue folder. He raced off the platform behind the auctioneer.

Apple was enraged. His blush disappeared, clicking off like a busted lamp. As an uproar came alive, surprise over, he pushed into the aisle and charged downhill.

Slamming aside those who got in his way (saying an excuse-me in his head), Apple reached the front and threw himself into a leap which, he being long of leg, finished in neat success.

The two guards were struggling up to their feet. Apple spared the second and a half necessary to give a potent shove to each, sending them down again. As he ran off, with the auctioneer moving hastily aside, thuds told him that others were hitting the platform steps.

Apple came into a type of backstage. There was a catholic selection of clutter, shapes of charm and menace in a dimness. Denver Campbell was ahead, dodging his way toward where dim graded to dark.

Rage cooling, Apple followed.

He vaulted on and off a grand piano, made another shortcut over a pile of rolled-up carpets, circled a rocking-chair which was still cavorting from Campbell's push and which he swiveled behind him as an impeder to the stampede behind.

The man ahead dissolved into darkness.

That was soon over. Even as Apple was slowing because of the reduced visibility, he saw an oblong of light come into upright being. It was a doorway. A shape passed through it and it then disappeared.

Apple stumbled on. A brief glance back showed him, beyond the several figures moving this way, a tableaux by the entrance to the platform: Bullybeef holding over his head one of the guards, whom he was about to throw at the other.

Coming to a wall, Apple fumbled for a handle, found one, turned it and yanked the door open. He shot out into a street, where, arms and legs spread like someone who had just jumped from a bedroom window, he looked about him in fast darts. He saw Denver Campbell.

On the roadway's other side, blue folder held in his teeth, the Scot was in the act of jumping into the saddle of the pedal-bike he was pushing at a run.

Apple was prevented from racing across by a passing bus. He ran beside it, crossing when it drew ahead. He found himself beside another runner, a man bristly with anger, whom he took to be the bicycle's owner. If there was one thing Apple didn't need, it was more competition.

They exchanged a glance. Apple grated, "If you catch up first—hold on to him tight."

"I know what to do."

"He's wanted for murder."

"I know what to do," the man said again before he fell back, limping.

Denver Campbell was drawing steadily away. Scanning as he gave chase, Apple saw no means of transport he could make use of—until, following around the first corner, he caught up with a pre-teen girl on a pre-teen bike.

Apple's hesitation was curt. Grabbing the girl firmly by the waist, he lifted her up in the air. The bike sailed sedately on and, for a moment, the girl's legs continued to circle, which Apple found rather endearing.

Setting her down near the kerb, he hissed gibberish at her while nodding with authority. Head craned far back, she gazed up at him with so much trust in her eyes that, hurt, he delayed, lingered to say an unexpected, "Sorry." She smiled.

The pounding of footfalls tore Apple away. Turning to hare after the bicycle, he saw that someone was there ahead of him. It was Tyrol. He snatched up the bike as it was falling, jumped on and pedalled off.

As Apple ran in pursuit, it was soothing to his feeling of outrage that Tyrol looked ludicrous on the small bicycle, his sharp-bent out poked legs furiously whirling. When Apple came within a slice of recognising the soother as relief (the person playing clown was not himself), he looked behind to check on the field.

Passing where the owner of Denver Campbell's machine had stopped to talk with the owner of Tyrol's, were what seemed to be a dozen scattered hounds, most on foot, two in a car that was hindered by that same foot traffic, one on a motor scooter that couldn't get by the car.

Prominent were Tilda, Double, tanned-blond Susan, the hairless man who had tried abduction in a taxi, Falcon, Wiley and some of those familiar faces.

Before he turned front again, Apple's last image was of the two bicycle owners. He just hoped there was no misunderstanding, that's all, hoped it would be clear to the girl who was, and who was not, the murderer.

The men on bikes were drawing rapidly ahead and

the first was leaving the second behind. Apple, running full out, had nearly started to see the situation as serious when it made a sudden change.

The truck came out of a side street. It happened at the same moment that Denver Campbell, confident in his distance, was taking a careful look back, the blue folder still clamped in his teeth. He rode straight into the truck's side.

The folder shot free, Campbell went over the handlebars, the truck stopped, Campbell's head hit metal, the bike collapsed, the trucker leaned out screaming about damage to his vehicle, Campbell fell white of face onto the tarmac.

For a big man, Tyrol was inordinately quick. Even as the Scotsman was landing, he was running forward after having swerved to a stop and ditched his machine in the middle of the road. At a spanking dash he picked up the folder and went around the truck's rear.

Apple reached the small bicycle. Continuing the scythelike swing of his lift, he set it down again between a pair of parked cars. As he nimbled around behind the truck, its driver was getting down with the sworn intention of beating Denver Campbell into a mush.

There was a bus. It was moving on from a stop. Tyrol, his hat still neatly in place, the blue folder gripped in one hand, was racing to catch up. He did so. As he jumped aboard at its rear door, the bus slowed.

Apple, who himself had been slowing when he saw no hope of catching up on foot, speeded up again. With his scalp going *ting* with success, he reached the door and fast alighted. The bus put on speed.

Apple slowed. Tyrol had also slowed. The cause of both was a police presence.

Stretched out along the bus aisle, straphanging, were

six or seven policemen. Although their insouciance of stance and their cigarettes stated that they were off duty, they were still policemen, and policemen had to live, too, pay bills, so were ever alert to possibilities that could lead to a career advance, and if these happened to be legitimate even, so much the better.

This Apple explained to himself on noting how carefully the law officers were weighing up the two passengers who had arrived ruffled and grim, but who now were smiling and calm and torpid.

Showing expensive dental work, Tyrol, having passed the first policeman, was edging slowly past the next. He moved as though with reluctance. He was in no hurry whatever. He had all the time in the world. He had no place to go in particular. He was so harmless it was a treat.

Apple was cut from the same wonderful cloth, a bolt of heavenly blue, he hoped to imply as, smiling, he sidled by the first officer, who looked at him as you would at a pauper after your daughter.

Apple had succeeded in getting safely by when a clatter announced that the bus, which was slowing and spurting in traffic, had collected another new passenger. Keeping it casual, Apple glanced back.

Panting and intense, Susan gathered herself together from the alarm of boarding. She took fast measure of the scene. Then, blinking brightly like a toddler at the merry-go-round, she put on a dreamy smile and started to move forward. She went at a dawdle.

Apple went on. While he was scraping past a watchful, frowning officer at the speed of regret, his lips pursed in a breathy whistle to show his lack of concern, he recalled that he was carrying a gun.

The weapon wasn't loaded, true, but Apple had to

point out that he was also in possession of the bullets, which in law amounted to almost the same thing. Either way, if he were searched, he would be detained, held until he could sort things out, meaning good-bye to the manuscript.

At his stupidity in not having gotten rid of the gun, Apple pinked. Being that the blush was light, he remembered his latest antidote.

You had to imagine you were trapped in a sauna, advised Matron Kelly in a plain envelope from Southend-on-Sea. You were fully dressed as well as wearing a woollen hat and boxing gloves, former so low as to interfere with your vision, latter no help in your efforts to get the door open. When faced with such mammoth levels of panic and heat, your blush would fade in embarrassment.

Sauna alone without frills was all Apple needed now to cool off, get him moving again from where he had halted in front of the policeman, whose frown had increased. In leaving, Apple gave him a comfortable nod.

Before tackling the next stage, Apple looked back. He was no longer of interest to the officer, who, about to be brushed past by the willowy Susan, was accordingly taking up a little more space in the aisle.

Beyond that, a new passenger had just burst hectically inside. It was Baldy, the hairless would-be abductor. Twitches rippling over his heavy features, he took in the situation at speed. His last twitch became the first move toward creating a smile, which was in full stretch by the time he started to lag forward.

Apple went on. Tyrol, he noted grimly, was drawing ever closer to the front exit. If he got out, that could spell finis for those left on the bus, which, therefore, had to be brought to a stop.

And, Apple thought on in a rush, if the stop could be made sudden, unexpected, that would throw everyone off balance, including Tyrol but excluding the stopper, who could grab the folder and take off.

Excellent, Apple mused. But there was no emergency cord as in a train, and bus drivers generally took pride in how completely they could ignore the bell. There would have to be another way.

Apple asked: What about a gunshot? A scream? A missile to the driver's head? A fight with a cop? A shrieked protest from one of the female passengers? A violent seizure?

The last two Apple found curiously attractive. Which, somehow, let him know they wouldn't be the best of choices. Therefore it was between the others. He weighed:

Fight, no, it could take too long and finish with fighter arrested. Missile, maybe. Gunshot, no, since the gun would first have to be loaded, and in concealment. Scream, perhaps. So, gun and fight were out, and as hitting the driver, an innocent party, would be grossly unfair, the answer seemed to be a scream.

Apple was beside a pair of policemen. Both were watching him with heads tilted to suit the difference in heights and with faces a shade averted. Their eyes darted ahead to Tyrol and behind to the other two, as though trying to divine a connexion between the four smiling creepers.

Without warning, almost without giving himself advance notice, Apple exploded into sound. His screamed word was *stop*, his language French, his mode the imperative.

Results started even as the noise was still battering around windows and low roof.

The bus lurched into a brake-grinding slur. Two women passengers shot to their feet with yells of fear. People cried out. The pair of nearby officers, faces snapping to stark, jerked mightily on their straps. Their colleagues were likewise saved by being straphangers. But Tyrol was flung with force against the front, Susan and Baldy were hurled into forward staggers, and Apple, who had forgotten about holding on, was thrown to the floor.

There followed some seconds of confusion. What immediately concerned Apple was being trampled over by Susan, fallen on by Baldy, accidentally kicked by the two policemen as they moved away and by a man who was trying to leave his seat.

Cursing the innate biblical-sensing thoroughness which had made him unthinkingly put megaphonesque hands to his mouth for the scream, probably, Apple looked up.

Still recovering, one leg raised, Tyrol had his back on the windshield. His arms were stretched out front for balance. One hand held the blue folder, which Susan now plucked neatly away. Turning to the door, she leapt outside.

The confusion graded up, becoming bedlam. During the time Apple spent getting to his feet, after twice being thrust down again, he was aware of shouter battling shouter for verbal prominence. The matter ranged from a cry for help to a call for solidarity against terrorism, from a female's repeat ordering of a Marcel *chéri* to stay out of it to a male's harsh question of why the authorities didn't get tough.

Everyone seemed to be involved, voice or body, with the exception of Apple. The officers from the back had gone forward, above him, so that as he began reversing when erect, there was no one around but passengers. They had the same view as Apple:

Baldy, several policemen, Tyrol, the driver, and a man perhaps called Marcel all milling and snarling in a mélange of turmoil, with others fretfully on the hover.

When, coming level with the rear door, Apple fell out, it was merely in his mind's eye. So strongly did he fear becoming, like some of the Competition, a figure of farce, that he was warning himself with pictures. He alighted sedately.

Looking about, the only known faces he could see were in the trailing distance. He skirted the bus, went to its front. Ahead he saw a car. It would have meant nothing to him had there not been that reverse outrider. Following the car on a motor scooter was Wiley, who was wigless.

Glad he had all along figured the Oriental as a shrewdy, Apple set off in chase. He felt confident. One, he would be able to take over the scooter from Wiley; two, the car was making poor speed in the evening traffic; three, if he caught up, he would try the routine of covering the windshield with his body, obliging the driver to stop.

Which driver, Apple saw as the car took a sharp right, was Double, still in his hair mask. The backseat held Falcon and Susan.

Wiley had been so close in his tailing that, when the car turned, he went straight on. He hadn't yet managed to bring his scooter to a halt as Apple, tutting at his ally's error, himself reached the corner and charged around it in a wide arc that didn't interfere with his rhythm.

The car was closer, slowed by a van. Apple ran harder. Thrilled, he gained, gained and gained, until he arrived at the car's back. He rapped efficiently on the roof.

As one, the three people inside swung their heads, a mass movement so neat that Apple had a blink of regret at not having been a part of it.

Fractionally, the car slowed. It was enough. Not wasting time on door-handles (the occupants, being pros, would have the doors locked), Apple shot to the front and threw himself onto the sloping windshield.

His head was near the driver and he began to dodge it about as or obstruction to vision while Double shifted his own head to see over, around or under. Annoyingly, he didn't look particularly put out. Neither did the two passengers.

Cool and ruthless, that's what they were, Apple thought, feeling less thrilled. They would let him stay there until they were out of town and speeding, when a swerve would send him flying off—to injury or death.

A swerve came now. It was not, however, severe enough to budge Apple even slightly. He saw that they had turned off the street and were going down a concrete ramp, where high-rises towered above. The pace was leisurely. He sat up.

The small area in which the car came to a gentle stop was the service yard behind a cinema. In the gloom created by buildings and the approach of dusk were garbage-cans and bottle crates and a discarded popcorn machine.

Double switched off the engine. He and the others opened doors and started to alight, their manner relaxed, satisfied, as smooth as a hum of victory.

Apple got off the car. Warily he positioned himself for action, hoping to give the impression that he knew what he was doing, as Double came toward him at a menacing loll.

Settling his fur collar closer to his neck, Falcon broke the silence. He said, "If you stand aside peaceably, Mr. Walter Brent, you will not get hurt."

"I want that manuscript."

"Sorry."

Apple made a move forward. He didn't see the Double-sent punch that caught the point of his chin, though he felt it as a second pain. The first one was when the back of his head hit a wall. He stood there in a dreamy droop.

Along with a muttered order, Falcon snapped his fingers. Susan tossed the blue folder to the ground.

Everybody looked around as, with a roar, Wiley arrived. Squeezing past the car, skidded across the space where stood the group and with effort avoided hitting Double in the back. His stop was partly due to a garbage-can, partly to slushy brakes. He killed the motor, got off and pointed at Double with, "You're an impostor."

Apple told him, "Never mind that."

Wiley next pointed at the manuscript. "That's my property."

"Not really," Falcon said. "It belongs, one could say, to the world. Carry on, my dear."

Susan squatted beside the folder. She had a box of matches. She took one out and struck a light. After flickering in the faint breeze, the flame died.

In a hollow-sounding voice like an echo, Wiley asked, "What on earth are you doing?"

Suavely Falcon said, "Destroying the manuscript."

"Why?"

"It is an attack on Mr. Sherlock Holmes. An attack born either of forgery or the author's failing mind."

Apple, not knowing whether to be surprised or not, but pretending he wasn't, said, "That happens to be a rare piece of English literature."

"English?" Falcon said. "Only partly. As is well know and widely accepted, the author, Sir Arthur Conan Doyle, was born in the Soviet Union."

You people would believe anything you read in *Pravda*, Apple almost said.

Susan had opened and upended the folder, so that the manuscript was formed like a roof, the edges of its pages against the ground.

Having stopped wincing at this solecism, Wiley threatened, "I'll fetch the police."

Amiably, Double told him, "Try leaving."

Apple leaned away from the wall, felt dizzy, leaned back again. He told himself he was busy trying to think of a plan to rescue the manuscript.

As Susan was striking another match, two more people arrived to join the gathering. One was Tyrol and the other Baldy. Both dishevelled, they stopped by the car front and raised their eyebrows at the flame that Susan held against one of the pages.

"Don't just stand there," Apple snapped at the newcomers. "Do something."

Tyrol said, "I'm outnumbered."

In guttural English, Baldy said, "So am I."

Tyrol, taking off his hat: "It will be a tragic loss."

Baldy, cheerfully: "It will indeed."

"For me particularly," Tyrol said. "Conan Doyle was an honorary citizen of Reichenbach, you know."

"That is not proved," Baldy said. "What is true is that Doyle secretly became a citizen of Albania."

"There are three of us," Apple told them. Generously he added Wiley. "Four. Let's jump this guy who's been impersonating me. Okay?"

As Tyrol was explaining how he had hurt his back on the bus windshield and Baldy was offering that he was sure he had sustained internal injuries when disabling three policemen, more people arrived.

Bullybeef, Tilda and Mimi pushed through to the front, followed by two men with familiar faces. On seeing the flame that was growing on the manuscript page, all five subsided with expressions of contentment.

Giving a frustrated squeal, Wiley ran forward. He was pushed by Double, pushed again by Falcon, grabbed by Baldy, who held on and told him, "We are outnumbered, alas."

Wiley looked across at Apple with an appeal. He said, "Please." His tone was a throb of true, profound, bibliophilic anguish.

Apple discovered he was no longer able to ignore the moral question which had been keeping him from recalling that he was in possession of a gun with which he could turn tables here and save the manuscript.

What he could do once he had saved it, Apple thought as he leaned off the wall, to avoid Angus Watkin's plans on destruction, was preserve it for prosperity by leaving it with his lawyer to be exposed only after his death, but telling Watkin he had put it to the torch.

"Do something, somebody," Wiley pleaded from where he was being firmly held by Baldy, looking his appeal around the group. "It's not too late."

It was a second's work for Apple to whip out the gun. He gestured with it. "Nobody move."

Move everyone did, but only to tense and straighten

and lose complacency like drinkers struck sober. Falcon said a soothing, "Now now, Mr. Walter Brent."

Two more people arrived, one after the other. The first was Denver Campbell, the second Linda. Both pushed through to the foreground and stared at the burning manuscript.

Apple looked at Wiley, ordering, "Come here. Take this gun. If anyone tries to stop me—shoot."

Linda said, "Good for you, Wally-o."

When the Oriental, getting free of Baldy, had shakily taken over as gunman, Apple stepped to the folder. He was pleased as Linda went to Wiley with, "I think I'd be better at this than you."

"Yes," Wiley said, giving her the gun.

Apple lifted the burning manuscript. He held in a stoop, on the lip of blowing, when Linda said in a hard voice, "Put it back down, sport."

"What?"

"You heard. Put it down and let it go on burning."

"I don't think so."

"Then I'll blast your elbow."

Apple said, "The gun isn't loaded."

She aimed at his leg. "Let's give it a try."

"Okay okay, it's loaded."

"So put the manuscript down."

Obeying, stepping back, Apple told himself that for all he knew it could be true about the gun, since he hadn't counted the bullets when he had taken them out. And he couldn't accuse himself later of not having tried. But he still didn't know the answer to his moral question, which essentially was one of loyalty.

The flames took hold on the folder, lighting up the dim area prettily. People edged closer, forming a rough circle. Denver Campbell, putting out his hands to the fire, exchanged nods with Falcon.

He said, "This is most unfortunate."

"All forgeries must perish."

Wiley self-consoled, "It could be that, yes."

Denver Campbell said, "My associates, the Ancient Hibernian Society, will be disappointed. As everyone knows, Sir Arthur had a Scottish mother."

"I beg your pardon," Linda said, still holding the gun prominent, "his mother was Jewish."

Well well, a Mosad-maid, Apple had already started to muse before it came to him that, of course, this couldn't be so. Linda was no more Israeli secret service than Baldy was Albanian or the others what they hinted at being.

As they were all intelligence operatives and were all recognised by the others as such, even if they were willing to blow cover to each other with claims to Conan Doyle through citizenship or parentage, they wouldn't do so in front of outsiders Wiley and Walter Brent, who would carry the tale. If you were going to be a party to literary sacrilege, you couldn't beat putting the blame on an enemy. So Linda was probably working for the Arabs and Falcon's team were surely CIA.

Which, Apple thought, was nice to know but no help with his question.

As he squatted and held his hands toward the flames, whose slow advance said there was still time, Apple heard one of the familiar types telling Mimi, "Doyle's mother, in actual fact . . ."

And writing's mother, Apple thought, was philology. Did his loyalty, therefore, lie with Literature? Or should it be given to Upstairs, the organization he had sworn to serve? Or was it better used to save the reputation of a universally loved giant of fiction? Or was it only decent to give it to seeing that the wishes of the deceased author were followed?

Responsibility for that last, Apple decided, lay with no one other than the Doyle estate. And as to the bubble reputation, that could be bought or sold for a song, and it wasn't his place to play the singer.

Apple looked into the flames. The matter of loyalty, he saw, seemed to rest on the question of which was of greater consequence, Literature or Espionage, which itself depended on the question of permanency, for man's obligation as a procreating animal was to look to the future with as much force as in his honouring of the past.

Espionage had a far longer history than Literature, longer almost than the word in its spoken form, Apple readily agreed; less readily, though bravely, he allowed that it was a history of corruption. Changing aims turned embraces to backstabs, enemies to dear comrades. It was a history created not by events but by politicians, whose decisions had precipitated those events, and politicians were not always the most honourable of men.

Espionage had a future, Apple knew. It would never die so long as there were two people left alive in the world, yet it couldn't change for the better because its betterment would be its death, a cloak rendered transparent, a dagger ground blunt.

Apple rubbed his hands together for the comfort, musing, Literature had a history of honour. It had informed, enlightened and enchanted more than it had perverted, hurt or dismayed. It would never die either, so long as there were two people alive, one to read, the other to bear future readers, and so long as neither was a politician.

Apple nodded at the flames. All well and good, he thought. But coming back to a personal level, he had made no promises to Philology or daughter Literature, whereas there was no avoiding the fact that he had sworn allegiance to Upstairs.

Apple looked around the circle. The fire's glow shone on faces that bore a pudginess of complacency. Even Wiley was less dejected, seemed to be accepting the forgery persuasions of Baldy and Tilda. The other two pseudo-Sickles were asking Linda about her seamstress, Bullybeef and Tyrol were exchanging cigarettes, one of the familiars was helping Double get out of his hairpiece, and Falcon was telling Denver Campbell about his lumbago.

Apple wondered how many of these spies were obeying orders. Most had to be disobeying, as their organizations could make little use of ashes. They were allowing destruction of the manuscript out of a personal feeling for a favourite hero, fictional though he might be.

Apple smiled. His mind made up, he rose. A man's loyalty belonged first and utmost to himself, he conceded, meaning that the wishes of Appleton Porter came before those of Agent One. Although there was still time to save part of the manuscript, a matter of greater urgency called for attention. Right at this moment a small bicycle might be undergoing theft or destruction. It had to be claimed and returned to its owner. At once.

Moving out of the circle, Apple headed for the concrete ramp. Linda called, "I wouldn't really have shot you, Wally-o. Don't go 'way mad."

"I'm not angry, Linda. You had a job to do. Later we'll have a drink together."

"Good. So where you going?"

Pausing to look back, Apple answered with a lie. He didn't realise he did so because he would rather be an inch taller than have the truth known; he didn't realise he chose this particular lie because it was the kind of reply he would have given if he were the person he longed to be; he assumed he was performing his cover role of the eccentric to the very end, as a pro should, when he said, casually, "To see if I can get some chestnuts."

About the Author

Marc Lovell is the author of eleven previous Appleton Porter novels, including *That Great Big Trenchcoat in the Sky* and *The Spy Who Barked in the Night*. *Apple Spy in the Sky* was made into the film *Trouble at the Royal Rose*. Mr. Lovell has lived for over twenty years on the island of Majorca.